"I didn't kill anyone."

"Never said you did," Rebecca replied smoothly. "I'm just laying out the facts here. It's one thing to stumble across one dead body. But to find two in two weeks? That's some exceptional luck."

"I wouldn't call it that," Quinn muttered.

"Neither would I," she said, her tone suddenly harsh. "What is it about you, Quinn Gallagher? Don't you find it odd that you've come across three—no, *four*—dead women in the last two years?"

"I hadn't thought of it like that," he faltered. For the first time, a kernel of fear took root in his chest. Was he really going to be blamed for the deaths of these women?

"Well, I have," she responded. "And let me tell you, it's one hell of a coincidence."

"I don't believe in coincidence," he said.

"Well, what do you know?" She leaned back and smiled broadly. "Neither do I."

* * *

If you're on Twitter, tell us what you think of Harlequin Romantic Suspense!
#harlequinromsuspense

Dear Reader,

Welcome to the Rangers of Big Bend series! I'm so excited to dive into this world! As a native Texan, I'm proud to set these stories in one of our most beautiful parks. I'm not much of a camper, but even I can appreciate the beauty of Big Bend—it truly is a special place.

Quinn and Rebecca are two weary souls faced with a terrible situation. It would be easy for them to let the circumstances further harden their protective shells, but against all odds, they find themselves working together with both their heads and their hearts. I hope you enjoy their journey, and be sure to return for the rest of the series!

Happy reading!

Lara Lacombe

RANGER'S JUSTICE

Lara Lacombe

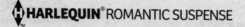
HARLEQUIN® ROMANTIC SUSPENSE

Recycling programs
for this product may
not exist in your area.

ISBN-13: 978-1-335-45656-4

Ranger's Justice

Copyright © 2018 by Lara Kingeter

This edition published by arrangement with Harlequin Books S.A.

For questions and comments about the quality of this book, please contact us at CustomerService@Harlequin.com.

HARLEQUIN®
™ www.Harlequin.com

Printed in U.S.A.

Lara Lacombe earned a PhD in microbiology and immunology and worked in several labs across the country before moving into the classroom. Her day job as a college science professor gives her time to pursue her other love—writing fast-paced romantic suspense with smart, nerdy heroines and dangerously attractive heroes. She loves to hear from readers! Find her on the web or contact her at laralacombewriter@gmail.com.

Books by Lara Lacombe

Harlequin Romantic Suspense

Rangers of Big Bend

Ranger's Justice

The Coltons of Red Ridge

Colton K-9 Bodyguard

Doctors in Danger

Enticed by the Operative
Dr. Do-or-Die
Her Lieutenant Protector

The Coltons of Shadow Creek

Pregnant by the Colton Cowboy

The Coltons of Texas

Colton Baby Homecoming

Deadly Contact
Fatal Fallout
Lethal Lies
Killer Exposure
Killer Season

Visit Author Profile page at Harlequin.com for more titles.

This one is for Dr. Kuban. Thanks for everything!

Prologue

She was very nearly perfect.

He stood over her, head cocked to the side as he ran his gaze over her still form. Limbs arranged just so, hair an artful tangle obscuring her face, one sightless eye playing peekaboo from between the strands. Yes. This would do.

He stripped off his gloves and shoved them into the bag at his feet. Walking over to a small shrub nearby, he broke off a dry branch and set about erasing the footprints he'd left in the sand. It was tedious, almost boring work, but it was important he destroy any evidence that might point in his direction. The police might catch him someday, but he still had much to do.

Finally finished, he stood on the rocky trail and

surveyed his work. Pride surged through him, along with a pang of regret. He wanted nothing more than to stay with her, to tell her all the secrets of his heart. But as much as he wanted to linger, it was too big of a risk. The first orange tendrils of dawn were streaking across the sky, and hikers started early in the park. Better for him to leave. She wouldn't be lonely long—someone would find her soon enough.

"Goodbye, lady," he whispered. He blew a kiss on the wind and smiled sadly. "I enjoyed our time together. I'll see you again."

With one final glance back, he turned and set off down the trail.

Park ranger Quentin "Quinn" Gallagher crested the small hill and paused, adjusting his hat against the glare of the morning sun. The ground was still cool from the night, but the air was warm and it wouldn't take long for the heat of the day to set in.

The trail in this section of the park was rocky and on an incline, and he stepped carefully as he set off again. He hadn't run into anyone so far, but that would likely change on his trek back. This was one of the more challenging trails in the park, and experienced hikers liked to test their mettle against the sloping switchbacks and narrow path. The reward for their determination was one of the best views in the park, which, in Quinn's mind, made up for all the work.

He enjoyed hiking for pleasure, but for today's journey he was focused on work. Yesterday, two campers had reported a section of safety railing was deteriorating to the point of falling down. Since the area in question was in an especially treacherous area, Quinn had volunteered to check it out today. He had a few supplies in his backpack, but if things looked as bad as the campers had described, he'd probably have to close the trail until they could bring a crew in to repair the damage.

The muscles in his legs burned pleasantly as he moved up the mountain. Big Bend National Park was no match for the Rocky Mountains, but the Chisos range was nothing to laugh at, either. The landscape changed as he made his ascent up Emory Peak, the low, green scrubland giving way to exposed rock. Small clumps of weeds sprouted tenaciously in the gaps between rocks, and he passed the skeleton of a rabbit, the bones bleached white from exposure. Quinn knew he was getting close as he spied the large solar panel and tall antennae at the top of the peak—the equipment was part of the two-way radio system employed by the Park Service in Big Bend. It wasn't the prettiest of additions, but the setup served an important purpose.

He rounded a curve and a flash of pink caught his eye. He paused, scanning the area again with a slight frown. The land in this part of the park was all browns and greens—pink was definitely not a normal part of the scenery. *Probably trash left behind by some hikers*, he thought sourly. Most people were respectful of nature and took pains to collect their debris, but there were always a few bad apples who couldn't be bothered to do the right thing. He peered against the glare of the sun, hoping to catch the flash of color again. A breeze drifted by, and he saw pink flutter in the wind. Over there—about twenty feet off the trail.

Quinn carefully moved off the trail, mindful of where he stepped so as not to cause too much damage to the landscape. As he approached, it looked like the pink was a bit of fabric caught on the branches of the bushes that dotted the area. Maybe a scarf, or perhaps a discarded jacket cast off by a hiker who got too hot on the trail.

He bent down to untangle the fabric and froze as he got his first good look at the spot. His body seemed to recognize what he was seeing before his brain registered the scene—the hairs on the back of his neck stood on end, and a chill swept over him.

"Oh, my God," he whispered. His stomach twisted violently, and he turned away as a wave of nausea propelled his breakfast up and out of his body. He retched into the bushes, then reluctantly turned back, his hand pressed to his mouth.

The woman was on her back, impossibly still, her arms bent at the elbows and hands resting over her heart. Her knees were bent and the soles of her feet were pressed together, leaving her legs splayed out in a grotesque parody of a yoga pose. She looked almost peaceful, except for the horribly tangled hair arranged across her face, obscuring her features. One cloudy blue eye was visible in a gap between the strands, staring lifelessly at the sky.

Quinn's heart pounded in his chest and blood thundered in his ears. For a moment, all he could do was stare at the body and try to comprehend what he was seeing. Working as a park ranger, he was no stranger to death—he'd come across the carcasses of animals from time to time, but that was just a part of nature. This—this was something else entirely.

He reached out and touched the side of her neck with his fingertip, feeling for a pulse he knew wasn't there. Still, he had to be sure.

Her skin was cold to the touch, her flesh unnaturally stiff under his finger. He snatched his hand back and rubbed it over his pants, trying to erase the feeling of death before it could fully take hold of him.

He closed his eyes as a memory assaulted him, filling his senses.

Ashley. His wife. Her body lying twisted on a different trail, bones broken from the fall that had taken her life.

A wave of helplessness made his knees buckle, and Quinn fell to the ground, tears streaming down his face. He had arrived too late to save Ashley. And now it seemed history was repeating itself.

Except… He frowned as his whirling thoughts began to settle. Ashley had fallen over the edge of a trail while hiking in Yosemite National Park, landing on a small outcrop twenty feet below. That didn't seem to be the case here. While the woman's body lay in a small declivity in the land, there was no overhang nearby, no cliff she might have tumbled off. It was as if she'd dropped from the sky, placed here by some unseen hand.

Murder.

The word appeared out of nowhere, a shout in his mind that cut through the fog of his shock and memories. He forced himself to really look at the body, searching for signs of injury or foul play. There was nothing obvious to see, but he knew without a doubt this woman had been killed.

His hand shaking, Quinn reached for his radio and called back to base to report this sad discovery. Given his position on the trail, it was going to take a couple of hours before anyone could reach him. Dispatch assured him the police were on their way, and Quinn resigned himself to the fact he was going to have to stay on the scene until they arrived. He moved back to the trail and hiked down to the closest switchback, then draped a rope across the trail and affixed a small Trail Closed sign to it. His fellow rangers would close off the trail at its start, but he wanted to make sure any hikers who had already set out wouldn't stumble across the scene.

With a sigh, he returned to the body. He didn't want to stay nearby, but it felt wrong somehow to leave her alone. He debated draping his light jacket over her face—he wanted to give her some dignity—but in the end he held back. If he touched her again or interfered with the scene in any way it would make it harder for the police to do their job.

Not knowing what else to do, Quinn sat a few feet away in the paltry shade of one of the bushes, keeping company with a dead woman and the ghost of his wife.

Chapter 1

Two weeks later

"Do I need a lawyer?"

Rebecca Wade paused in the doorway to the interrogation room, taken aback by the question. As a psychologist in the FBI's famous Behavioral Analysis Unit, she'd interviewed all sorts of men and women over the years. She had dealt with any number of threats, both overt and subtle, lies, tears, accusations, claims of innocence and a few attempted seductions during these conversations. Rarely were the people she talked to so direct right off the bat.

She closed the door behind her with a soft *snick*. "That depends," she said.

The man stiffened at the sound of her voice, and he turned around to face her. His eyes widened when he saw her. "You're a woman."

Rebecca lifted one eyebrow. "Is that going to be a problem?" Her mind was already whirring with possibilities. She was here to talk to him about the deaths of two women in Big Bend National Park. This ranger had found their bodies a week apart, making him a potential suspect in the murders. And if he was such a blatant misogynist, maybe this conversation wasn't going to take as long as she'd estimated.

"No, ma'am," he said. "Not a problem. Just a surprise." He pushed back the chair and stood, and Rebecca's body tensed. Was he going to attack? It wouldn't be the first time a suspect had come after her, and while she was confident in her self-defense skills, she didn't want to test them against this man. He was taller than her by a good six or seven inches, and he likely outweighed her by about forty pounds.

He must have read the tension on her face because he took a step back and gestured to the chair across from him. Rebecca kept her gaze on him as she took the long way around the table. Only when she had taken a seat did he sit back down, and she realized with a small shock that he had jumped to his feet in a display of manners rather than an attempt to scare her.

Interesting.

"As I was saying, Mr. Gallagher, you're not under arrest. You are free to have a lawyer present during our conversation, but if you elect to do so, I won't talk to you until your counsel arrives." It made no difference to her what he decided. She'd talked to plenty of guilty men who had rejected an attorney because they thought they were smarter than her. Conversely, the innocent often asked for a lawyer, just to make sure they didn't get into unnecessary trouble. Either way, she couldn't read too much into his choice.

He was quiet, his expression thoughtful as he considered her words. She took the opportunity to study his face. He was handsome, she could say that objectively. Long, straight nose, tousled hair and brown eyes that looked like twin pools of melted chocolate framed by long lashes. The dusting of stubble on his cheeks kept him from looking too boyish. There were faint lines at the corners of his mouth and eyes, indicating he probably smiled a lot. She was willing to bet he had dimples when he did.

Yes, a handsome man. One a woman wouldn't think twice about talking to, especially if he turned on the charm. It would probably be easy for him to gain a woman's trust.

But did that make him a killer?

Finally, he shrugged. "Let's just get this over with," he said. "I have nothing to hide."

That's what they all say, Rebecca thought.

"My name is Rebecca Wade. I'm an agent in the FBI's Behavioral Analysis Unit, and the Alpine police have asked me to talk to you about the women you found in Big Bend." Alpine was a decent-sized city about a hundred miles from the borders of the park. The Alpine police was taking point on the investigation because its members had resources some of the smaller, closer towns lacked.

He nodded, as if this was information he already knew. "You already have my name. But I'll introduce myself anyway. I'm Quentin Gallagher. Call me Quinn."

"All right."

"How does this usually work?" He shifted in the chair and it rocked a little in response, indicating the legs were not all the same length. Shortening the legs was a classic interrogation technique designed to keep the suspect uncomfortable and literally off balance. Rebecca wasn't convinced it worked all that well, but she wasn't going to argue with the Alpine police department about their methods right now.

"We're just going to talk," Rebecca said. "I have a few questions for you, but I'm mainly interested in hearing your story in your own words."

A shadow crossed Quinn's face, as if he was remembering something especially troubling. He cleared his throat. "Where should I begin?"

"Tell me about your wife."

"My wife?" Quinn asked, his voice cracking a little on the words. Rebecca watched his face carefully, noting how his skin went pale under his tan. "What would you like to know about Ashley?"

"How did you two meet?"

He hesitated, and for a brief second, Rebecca wondered if he had changed his mind about talking to her. *Maybe opening with his wife was a mistake*, she mused. But if so, she had other tricks up her sleeve. One way or another, she was going to get Quinn Gallagher's story.

Just as she was about to try another tack, Quinn spoke.

"I'll tell you whatever you want to know," he said quietly. "But before we get started, I need you to understand something." His brown eyes shone with an emotion she couldn't quite name, and he leaned forward a bit, his expression earnest.

"Okay," she said agreeably. "What's that?" She was careful to keep her tone neutral, but her heart rate picked up. Was he really going to confess so quickly? It normally took her hours, or even days, to coax a confession from a suspect. Maybe Quinn was going to make it easy on her…

He met her eyes, his gaze intense, as if he was trying to see her very soul. Rebecca resisted the temptation to look away and tried to appear friendly and interested in what he had to say. It was important to gain Quinn's trust so he would open up to her. The faster she got him to let down his guard, the sooner she'd discover the truth.

"I didn't kill those women in the park." His voice was low, but he enunciated every word clearly, as if he wanted to make sure she didn't misunderstand him.

"And I damn sure didn't kill my wife."

If Quinn's words shocked Rebecca, she didn't show it. She smiled slightly, and he got the impression this wasn't the first time she'd heard a man proclaim his innocence.

But in his case, it was the truth.

"If I really thought you'd killed anyone, you'd already be under arrest," she said smoothly.

Yeah, right, he thought. Quinn wasn't stupid. The only reason he wasn't in handcuffs right now was because the police didn't have enough evidence to charge him with the murders of those two unfortunate women he'd found in the park. Finding the first body had been bad enough. Finding the second victim, a week later, on a different trail, had been a new level of horrible. He knew he was still a suspect, though. Actually, the term the detective had used was "person of interest," as if that was supposed to make him feel better.

It didn't.

Nothing about this situation was okay. The only thing that made it tolerable was the fact that he knew with absolute certainty there wouldn't be any evidence linking him to the deaths of those women.

Once the police realized he was innocent, these "voluntary" conversations would come to an end.

But until that day, Quinn intended to cooperate. The memories of his gruesome discoveries demanded he do everything in his power to ensure those poor women found some kind of justice.

The FBI interrogator was watching him, her face completely calm with no hint of impatience. She looked like a woman without a care in the world, as if she was happy to spend all day sitting in front of him, waiting for him to start talking. Her calm demeanor was a skill that likely served her well in her job, and under different circumstances, Quinn would have asked her more about her career. Working for the FBI had to be exciting, or at the very least, interesting.

Now was not the time for pleasantries, though.

Quinn took a deep breath, bracing himself for the jolt of pain that always came whenever he thought of Ashley. "We met in college," he began. "We had a couple of intro classes together. I noticed her on the first day, and after a few weeks, I finally worked up the nerve to talk to her." He smiled briefly at the memory, remembering the way his knees had practically knocked together as he'd stood in front of her desk and asked how she was doing.

He shook himself free of the memory and continued. "I was so nervous around her that if it had been up to me, I'd probably still be searching for the courage to ask her on that first date. Fortunately, Ashley was braver than I was, and she took matters into her own hands. She asked me to dinner, and I said yes. Four years later, we got married a week after graduation."

"Were you happy together?" Rebecca's voice was quiet and unobtrusive, the question a gentle conversational nudge to steer him in the desired direction. He knew where they were headed, and he swallowed hard.

"She was my everything," he said, his throat tight.

"Ashley was unique. She was insatiably curious, so full of life. Being around her was like holding lightning in your hands—she had so much energy and spark. Her personality was magnetic, and it was impossible not to be drawn in, to want to get close to her. When she looked at me, I felt like I was her whole world." Quinn paused and shook his head. "She certainly was mine."

"What did she look like?"

Ashley's face popped into his head, the image crystal clear even though he hadn't seen her in two years. "A little like you, actually," he said, glancing over Rebecca's features. "Red hair, pale skin, full lips. She had the most beautiful smile…" He trailed off, unable to continue. Not a day passed that he didn't think about her and the life they should have had together. Knowing he would never see her again was a special kind of torture, and Quinn often wondered if he'd ever be able to think about Ashley without pain. He knew she wouldn't have wanted him to suffer like this. Their time together and the year and a half they'd spent married had been so full of happiness, it seemed wrong to have it overshadowed by his grief. But he'd learned the hard way he couldn't control his emotions, no matter how he tried.

"She sounds very special," Rebecca said quietly.

Quinn nodded. "She was," he agreed.

"I know this is difficult for you, but will you tell me how she died?"

He'd known the question was coming, but it still

hit him like a punch to the gut. His eyes stung, and he blinked rapidly, determined not to shed tears in front of a stranger. Just because she looked like Ashley didn't mean she was Ashley, and he couldn't let Rebecca's appearance distract him now.

"Ashley loved to go hiking. It was something we both enjoyed, and we took a lot of camping trips together. She was so happy when I got assigned to Yosemite as my first ranger job—she always said it was her favorite national park." He smiled briefly at the memory.

"One of her friends had come out for a weekend visit. They had planned a hike on one of the more advanced trails, but since they were both experienced hikers, I didn't worry about them. Ashley and Naomi knew what they were doing, and they weren't the kind to take unnecessary risks with their safety. I had planned to go with them, but I was unexpectedly called in to work. I dropped them off at the trailhead and said I'd try to meet up with them later."

Rebecca nodded. She probably knew these details already—it was the same thing he'd told the police at the time. He knew it was her job to make him tell the story again, but that didn't make it any easier.

Quinn took a deep breath. Might as well get on with it. Drawing it out would only make him feel worse.

"After a few hours, my boss told me I wasn't needed anymore and I could go. I called Ashley and got her coordinates, and told her I'd meet her at one of the waterfalls that was a landmark along the trail. I knew a shortcut and set off. But when I got to the meeting point, they weren't there. I waited around a few minutes, thinking maybe they'd stopped for pictures or a water break. But when they still didn't show, I grew worried. I called Ashley's phone again, and that's when I heard it."

"Heard what?"

"Ashley's phone. I could hear it ringing. The sound came from somewhere below the trail." His gut twisted at the memory, and he heard the echo of her cheerful ringtone in his mind.

"I… I walked to the edge of the trail and saw…" He trailed off, unable to continue.

"They had fallen?" Rebecca asked softly.

Quinn nodded. His throat tightened up, and he didn't think he'd be able to go on. He forced out the words, and they scraped against his tongue as he spoke. "They were too far down for me to get to them. I yelled to them, but neither one responded. I called for a medical evacuation right away." The wait for the rescue crew had been the longest stretch of his life. He'd stared down at Ashley's still form, unable to look away, straining to see any small movement, any twitch that would indicate she was still alive.

"The police questioned you after your wife and her friend were recovered?"

"Yes." Quinn turned his thoughts away from that horrible discovery and focused instead on the aftermath. The small interrogation room, not unlike this one, where he'd sat, talking to the detectives.

"Why were you considered a suspect?" She sounded genuinely curious, even though she had to have read his file before walking into the room. Quinn thought about asking her the same question, but decided to humor her with a reply.

"Ashley and Naomi were experienced hikers, and the trail was in good condition," he said again. "It was determined they had most likely slipped over the edge, probably after getting too close for a photo. But I guess the police had to consider foul play, and since I was the last person to talk to Ashley, that made me a potential suspect."

"But they never arrested you."

"There was no evidence," he said simply. "I told you before, I didn't kill my wife or her friend. No matter how hard the police looked, they weren't going to find any evidence to the contrary."

Rebecca was silent a moment, considering his words. "When did you ask to be transferred?"

"About a week later. I couldn't continue to work at Yosemite—it was too hard."

"So you were assigned to Big Bend National Park about two years ago."

Quinn nodded. "It was a good change. Ashley would have loved it here, too, but it's easier to go to work knowing I'm not going to be ambushed by a sudden memory of us hiking this trail or camping in that spot."

Rebecca smiled. "I can imagine." She leaned back in her chair, her head tilted to the side. "I take it you enjoy your job?"

"I do. Very much."

"And you're feeling comfortable here? Like it's home?"

"Yes." *Where is she going with this?* Quinn wondered.

"Let's talk about the women you found."

The images flashed across his mind and he winced. "I don't know how much I can tell you," he said. "Like I told the police, when I found each woman, I called it in right away."

"I'm sure you did," Rebecca said soothingly. "I just want to know what you think about the situation."

Quinn frowned. "What I think?" he asked. "I think it's terrible what happened to those women."

Rebecca nodded. "I agree with you. I also think it's quite interesting that a man who was considered a suspect in his wife's death was the one to discover these two victims."

Quinn's blood ran cold as Rebecca continued. "Another thing that fascinates me is the fact that your wife had red hair. Do you remember the hair color of the women you discovered?"

"Red," he whispered, his mouth dry as the desert.

"That's right." She nodded, looking like a proud teacher pleased with her student's progress. "Red. Kind of a striking feature, wouldn't you say?" She leaned forward, as if she wanted to impart a secret.

"See, in my line of work, we call that a pattern. It's quite common for killers to target people who share a set of characteristics—in this case, hair color."

"I didn't kill anyone."

"Never said you did," Rebecca replied smoothly. "I'm just laying out the facts here. It's one thing to stumble across one dead body. But to find two in two weeks? That's some exceptional luck."

"I wouldn't call it that," Quinn muttered.

"Neither would I," she said, her tone suddenly harsh. "What is it about you, Quinn Gallagher? Don't you find it odd that you've come across three…no, *four* dead women in the last two years?"

"I hadn't thought of it like that," he spluttered. For the first time, a kernel of fear took root in his chest. Was he really going to be blamed for the deaths of these women? There wasn't any evidence linking him to the crimes, but the way Rebecca was talking made him second-guess his actions.

"Well, I have," she responded. "And let me tell you, it's one hell of a coincidence."

"I don't believe in coincidence," he said.

"Well, what do you know?" She leaned back and smiled broadly. "Neither do I."

"What do you think?"

Rebecca rolled her head to the side, stretching out her neck. It had been a long few hours in the interrogation room, and she was ready for a fresh cup of coffee.

She turned to the detective who'd asked the question. *Morris, that's his name*, she recalled.

"He's not a killer."

Detective Morris snorted and shook his head. "Just like that? You talked to him for what, two hours, and suddenly you know he's innocent?"

Rebecca gave him a level stare. "I know he didn't kill those women. He was on patrol with a partner when the medical examiner estimates both women were killed, which makes for a pretty good alibi, don't you think? Not to mention, he's not at all interested in the details of the deaths—he shut down hard when I started talking about it. That's not consistent with the behavior of a killer. They tend to enjoy hearing about their crimes. Gives them a chance to relive the excitement."

Morris nodded. "I've heard that."

"He's not the killer," Rebecca repeated. "But that doesn't necessarily make him innocent."

The man's eyes narrowed. "What do you mean?"

"I mean there's a possibility he's working with the killer. Pointing out potential victims, then 'discovering' them later so the killer can get his five minutes of fame."

"Like a wingman?"

Rebecca shrugged. "If that's what you want to call it."

"Why would a person want to do something like that?"

She sighed, suddenly exhausted. "There are any

number of reasons. But I just don't know if Quinn Gallagher is the type of man who would do such a thing." She glanced back at the door to the interrogation room, replaying their conversation in her mind. Nothing he'd said had triggered any alarm bells, but it would probably take several interviews for her to pick up on more subtle cues.

"Anything from forensics yet?"

Morris shrugged. "Not really. Fibers and fingerprints are still being processed. They did say the first scene was fairly pristine, while the second was more compromised."

"So he probably found the first body soon after she'd been dumped, while the second one sat there longer, giving animals and the elements time to degrade evidence." Rebecca's tone was thoughtful as she incorporated this piece of information into her mental file on Quinn Gallagher. She made a note to look at the report on his wife's death, see if there were any similarities across the sites. It was a long shot, but perhaps there were some commonalities. Her gut told her he wasn't the killer, but she'd been wrong before…

"That's what the evidence techs said," Morris confirmed. He jerked his head in the direction of the interrogation room. "How do you suggest we proceed?"

"Cut him loose." Rebecca stood and caught a glimpse of Morris's surprised expression. "You don't have any evidence against him. There's no reason to hold him."

"You really think it's a good idea to let him back out there?"

"Why not? Either the man is innocent, in which case it's wrong to detain him. Or he's working with the killer, in which case he'll make contact with our perp. Just keep an eye on him."

"We don't have that kind of manpower," Morris protested. "We can't follow him all the time."

Her phone buzzed at her hip, signaling an incoming email. Rebecca glanced at the screen and shook her head. "Then I guess it's a good thing your boss requested my services for the next few weeks." She pocketed the device and smiled wryly. "I'll stay close to him while I'm here. In the meantime, I need to change my hotel reservations. It seems I'm going to be here for the foreseeable future."

Chapter 2

It wasn't a bad room, as far as hotels went. The bed was small and lumpy, the air conditioner louder than a jet engine. But the air was cool and there was a desk in the corner where she could spread out her files. She'd slept in worse places before.

Rebecca sat in the lone chair in the room, twirling up forkfuls of lo mein as she worked through her emails. Her boss, Franklin Jessup, had told her to stay in Alpine for the next week at least to provide assistance to the local police in their investigation. Normally, two dead women in two weeks wasn't the kind of thing that would register at the national level, but since she'd already been in El Paso for a forensic psychology conference, the request from Alpine PD had been easy to accommodate.

This one sounds right up your alley, Frank had written. He was right; Rebecca had made somewhat of a name for herself focusing on crimes against women. It was one area where she felt she could really make a tangible difference in people's lives. Women were so often the target of violence—any time she helped put a killer behind bars, she knew she was saving lives of his future victims.

She had to admit she was intrigued by these cases—two red-haired women found in a national park in the space of two weeks. It was a hell of a pace, even for a serial killer. The local police had already dubbed the suspect "the Yoga Killer," thanks to the characteristic arrangement of the bodies: hands over hearts, legs bent with the soles of their feet touching. She pulled up the crime-scene photos for another look, noting how each woman had been placed in exactly the same pose, even down to the sprawl of hair across their faces.

"So he doesn't want to look at you," she murmured, clicking through the images. That was interesting. It seemed the killer had no problem taking a life, but he didn't want to be confronted by the empty, accusing stares of his victims. Postmortem guilt, perhaps? Maybe he got caught up in the moment when he was hurting these women, only to be filled with remorse after the fact. The possibility suggested he had poor impulse control, but the situation was more complicated than that. Both scenes had been devoid of any obvious evidence, and the crime-scene techs had reported it looked like the killer had taken pains to sweep away his footprints. Initial analysis of the bodies had revealed no fingerprints or DNA, which meant whoever was doing this was careful and methodical. Still, Rebecca knew there was no such thing as the perfect murder. They'd find the clue that would bring this killer to justice, no matter how improbable it seemed now.

She just hoped they caught a break sooner rather than later.

A quick search of the FBI's national database revealed no other similar cases, either in active investigation or resolved. That meant the killer was just starting out, or his previous victims hadn't been discovered yet. It was possible the man had been working quietly for years, perfecting his approach. The fact that he hadn't left behind any visible clues suggested a seasoned professional, but it was also possible he was just a smart guy who had watched a lot of *CSI*. A search of the database for missing persons turned up a disturbing number of young women with red hair, but there didn't appear to be any clusters that might indicate the Yoga Killer had been practicing elsewhere before moving to the Big Bend area. Still, she downloaded the report and emailed it to one of the interns at the Bureau with instructions to search through the files and categorize any cases that might be connected. Serial killers didn't just sprout from the ether; this guy had a history. All she had to do was find it.

She picked at her dinner, the noodles now cold and congealing into an unappetizing glob. Her thoughts drifted toward the park ranger she'd interrogated today. Quinn Gallagher. The man had been forthright and seemingly honest in his responses to her questions, and her instincts told her he wasn't a killer. But she couldn't shake the feeling he'd held something back during their conversation, as if there were things he'd wanted to say but hadn't. His subtle reticence didn't make him a bad guy, but it did make her want to know more. She couldn't quite put her finger on why, but she knew in her bones that Quinn was the key to this investigation. The question was, did he know that as well? Was he truly innocent as he claimed, or was he keeping information from her out of a sense of fear or guilt?

Only one way to find out.

"You and me, buddy," she muttered. Quinn might not know it now, but he'd just acquired a new sidekick. Rebecca was going to stick to him like glue during the course of this investigation, and sooner or later, she'd find out what he was hiding.

Bulldog Becca, on the case. Brandon's voice drifted through her mind, making her smile even as she felt the old familiar pang in her heart. She and Brandon had both worked for the Behavioral Analysis Unit, and over time their relationship had blossomed from being coworkers to friends to lovers. The day he'd proposed had been one of the happiest of her life, and she'd poured her free time into planning their wedding and honeymoon, daydreaming about their life together and the future they would build.

For a short time, her life had been perfect. She had a job she loved, a man she was crazy about and a future of endless possibilities to enjoy. But it all came crashing down one spring afternoon two years ago.

Brandon had been working in a Virginia prison, and he was interviewing a man on death row who had been convicted of the murders of several children. A few cold cases matched his pattern, but he had never confessed. Brandon was trying to coax more information out of the prisoner in the hopes of bringing closure to the families of the missing kids. It was draining, thankless work, but Brandon was good at his job and seemed to have a knack for getting people to talk to him.

They were about halfway through the interview when a riot broke out in one of the common areas of the prison. The complex was locked down, and the guard who normally stayed in the room during interviews moved to the door, turning his back on Brandon and the convict.

The killer saw his chance and took it. In a matter of seconds, he'd overpowered the guard and grabbed the baton. Then he turned on Brandon, who had been helpless to defend himself against the brutal beating.

Rebecca's throat tightened as the facts of the murder ran through her head. She hadn't been able to look at the photos from the scene, and Brandon's body had been cremated, so she hadn't had to see the evidence of his violent death. But that didn't stop her imagination from trying to fill in the details.

Losing Brandon had shattered her heart, and she'd nearly quit her job. Coming to work every day, passing by his office on the way to her own—it had been too much for her battered psyche to bear. Frank had seen how close to the brink she was, and insisted she take a break.

"We're not going anywhere," he'd said. "But you need time to heal."

Rebecca had initially resisted. Rattling around alone in the apartment she and Brandon had shared did nothing to help her grief. So she'd packed a bag and headed to Austin to visit her parents. They'd welcomed her with open arms and instructions to stay as long as she wanted.

The first few days, Rebecca did little more than sleep. In her dreams, Brandon was still alive, still with her. The horror of his death couldn't find her while she slept, and unconsciousness became her refuge. Her rational, clinical mind recognized she was sinking deeper into depression, but she felt powerless to stop the descent. The disease sank its teeth into her soul, gripping her tightly in a destructive embrace as it pulled her farther away from her family, her friends. Her life.

If not for the actions of her mother, Rebecca didn't know if she would be where she was today. Cherice recognized what was happening to her daughter and pushed her to see a therapist. Rebecca initially refused, but her mom kept insisting, applying a potent combination of begging, cajoling and tough love until Rebecca agreed to an initial session.

"This isn't something you can simply will away," Dr. Varton said during their first visit. "And with your education and experience, you know that better than anyone."

Slowly, Rebecca began to confide in the man. She told him about Brandon, about her overwhelming grief. And how the depression was making her question her capabilities as a psychologist. If she couldn't trust her own mind, was she really qualified to work for the FBI?

It had taken time, but with the help of Dr. Varton and medication, she'd grown to accept that the depression was not her fault and it didn't invalidate her professional abilities or make her less of a person. Four months after Brandon's death, she returned to the FBI, ready to get back to work. She had a few rough days in the beginning, but as the months had passed, she found she was able to think about Brandon without feeling like she was standing at the edge of a fathomless black hole, playing chicken with the monster that lived in the depths.

Now, a year and a half later, the memory of his voice brought more comfort than sorrow. There would always be a part of her heart that wouldn't heal, a raw spot where Brandon had lived. But she was getting better about walling it off, protecting it from the slings and arrows of daily life. Still, it was times like now when she wished she could talk to him again, to pick his brain and discuss the case with him. He'd been the perfect sounding board, always helping her to see the pattern or challenging her to look at things from a different angle.

With a sigh, she closed the laptop and tossed the remains of her dinner in the trash. It was getting late and she needed to sleep—she'd already called Quinn's superiors and confirmed he was expected at work at seven thirty in the morning. She wasn't quite sure what a park ranger's job entailed, but tomorrow she was going to find out.

Quinn arrived at park headquarters the next morning, feeling far older than his thirty years. He hadn't slept well the night before. Every time he closed his eyes, he saw the two women he'd found in the park, and the memories haunted him. Finding the first had been bad enough. When he'd found the second a week later, he'd needed time off to cope. His boss had insisted he talk to a counselor, but it hadn't helped much. The shrink had suggested some meditation techniques and visualization exercises, but it seemed no matter what Quinn tried to think about, his brain always circled back to the women and, eventually, Ashley.

The distraction of work was his only refuge, but even that had its limits. He was desperate to get outside, to move his body and let his mind take a break. But he was also more than a little afraid of what he might find while patrolling the park.

On the advice of the Alpine Police Department, the rangers had posted notices throughout the area, advising hikers and campers of the recent deaths. The signs were carefully worded so as not to cause panic, but anyone who paid attention to the news would know about the gruesome discoveries in the park. The press hadn't affected tourism…yet. New campers arrived every day, their packs bulging and their spirits high. Quinn could only hope that the killer had moved on; he didn't think he could handle finding another body.

"Quinn." He turned at the sound of his name to find his boss, Gary Thompson, standing in the doorway to his small office. Gary beckoned Quinn over and gestured for him to take a seat across from his desk.

"How you holding up?" The older man's gray eyes were filled with genuine concern, and Quinn felt something in his belly loosen. He propped his hat on his knee and shrugged.

"I've been better." Should he tell Gary about his dreams and his trouble sleeping? Or would that make it sound like he couldn't handle his job? The thought of time off with nothing but his thoughts for company frightened him, so he kept his mouth shut.

"I imagine you have." Gary shook his head. "Hell of a thing, these murders. I've never seen anything like it in my fifteen years with the National Park Service."

Quinn was silent, mulling over his response. He really didn't want to talk about the details of what he'd seen, but Gary wasn't the type to gossip. "I hope they catch whoever did this soon," he said.

Gary nodded. "You and me both. I got a call last night from some lady with the FBI. Rebecca something. She wanted to know when you'd be at work today."

Nerves jangled in Quinn's stomach. The police had released him last night after he'd spoken with her. Had they changed their minds? Was she coming to arrest him?

Please, not here, he thought desperately. If he was arrested inside the ranger station, in full view of his colleagues and any park visitors, his career would be over.

"If you need to take time off to help with the investigation, you've got it."

It took Quinn a moment to register what Gary was saying. "I'm sorry?"

"The FBI lady made it sound like you were helping her with the investigation. If you need to take some leave, it's fine with me."

Quinn nodded slowly, his thoughts racing. What was Gary talking about? Rebecca had given no indication she wanted his help when they'd spoken yesterday. Was this some kind of trick, or was he simply overreacting? "I appreciate that," he said. "I'll talk to her and find out if it'll be necessary."

"We all want to catch this killer," Gary said, rising to his feet. Recognizing the conversation was over, Quinn stood as well. "As I told the police and this FBI agent, we'll do whatever it takes to help their investigation. You're one of my best rangers, but we can spare you for that."

"Thank you, sir." The praise was unexpected, and Quinn felt both pleased and humbled at the man's words. It was nice to know his work was appreciated, especially now when he was feeling so uncertain about things.

Quinn headed over to his desk and placed his hat next to his computer keyboard, then walked over to the coffeepot and poured himself a cup of the strong brew. He glanced at the large white board posted on the far wall as he returned to his seat. The board displayed a detailed map of the park, along with today's weather forecast, river conditions, campsite closings and any areas of concern or issues to note. Nothing unusual jumped out—the burn ban prohibiting campfires was in effect, and the trails where he'd made his discoveries were still closed to allow the police to finish gathering evidence. Other than that, it looked like they were in for another warm day.

The bell above the door jingled, indicating a new visitor. Quinn's desk was behind a partition, so he couldn't see who had walked in. But he heard her voice float through the room as she returned a greeting from the front-desk attendant.

"Hello. I'm looking for Quinn Gallagher."

"Let me check if he's in." The young woman who manned the desk poked her head around the corner, one

eyebrow raised in query as she made eye contact with
Quinn. He nodded, and she moved back to her station.

"Yes, ma'am. He'll be out in just a minute."

"Thank you."

Quinn took a moment to brace himself, drawing
in a deep breath. *She's not going to make a scene*, he
told himself. He didn't know what more she wanted
to talk about, but whatever the subject, he'd get her
out of the station so they could have a bit of privacy.
His coworkers were good people, but everyone was
curious about the case of the two dead women. He'd
rather not discuss things in front of an audience, however well-meaning they might be.

Grabbing his coffee, Quinn walked around the
partition to the larger visitor's lobby. He spied her
right away, and not just because the place was otherwise empty. She was quite a sight with her long red
hair pulled back into a glossy ponytail that seemed to
spark in the morning sun. A pair of jeans accentuated
the curve of her hips, and she wore a thin long-sleeved
shirt over a tank top. The casual look threw him for
a moment; the last time he'd seen her, she'd been a
buttoned-up professional woman in a suit. Today she
looked softer, more approachable. The kind of woman
he might ask out for dinner, if he was so inclined.

He shook his head, dismissing the thought. He'd
dated some in the aftermath of Ashley's death, but
nothing serious. And he certainly wasn't about to try
to go out with a woman who suspected him of murder.

He cleared his throat. "Morning," he said.

Rebecca turned to face him. "Hi," she said. She gestured to the informational poster hanging on the wall. "I had no idea the park is so big—it says here it's bigger than Yosemite."

Quinn nodded. "Yeah. A lot of people don't realize how much diversity is here. We have more bird species than any other national park."

A look of genuine surprise flashed across her face. "That's impressive," she said.

"I'm sure you aren't here to talk about our wildlife." He nodded at the partition and the desks beyond. "Want to come back?"

"Sounds good. Thanks."

He led her to his desk and snagged a chair so she could sit. "Coffee?"

Rebecca shook her head. "No, thanks. I already had my boost for the morning."

"How can I help you today?"

She glanced around before speaking, apparently wanting to make sure no one was listening. "I'd like you to take me to the sites where you discovered the bodies." Her voice was low, and he appreciated her discretion. Apparently, he wasn't the only one who cared about keeping things as quiet as possible.

A knot formed in his gut, but he nodded. "I can do that." He wasn't looking forward to going back to those spots, but it made sense she'd want to see the areas. "You know all the evidence has been removed, right?"

"Yes. But I still want to see them. I need to see what the killer saw and be in the space where he moved. It might give me more insight into him if I can walk in his footsteps."

She sounded matter-of-fact, but her words sent a chill down Quinn's spine. The last thing he wanted was to seek out the residue of evil that lingered in the land, but if she thought it would help her catch whoever had murdered those two women, he'd suck it up.

"When would you like to go?" He sounded reluctant even to his own ears, but if Rebecca noticed his tone, she didn't react to it.

"Today, if possible."

Quinn's eyebrows shot up and he ran his gaze over her attire again, this time evaluating her appearance for hiking. "Uh, do you have any hiking experience?"

She lifted one shoulder in a shrug. "A little. Why? Is there a problem?"

He tilted his head to the side. "Not necessarily. But I found the first woman off an advanced trail. It'll take us several hours to get there, and the terrain is pretty rugged. It's not the kind of hike you take on a whim."

"What about the second victim?"

"That trail is more accessible—it's rated moderate in difficulty. We can probably do that today, but we need to do some prep work first."

"I have a few water bottles in my car," Rebecca offered.

Quinn smiled for what felt like the first time in weeks. "That's a good start, but there's a bit more to it. Were you planning on wearing that?" He gestured to her jeans and sneakers.

She looked down and frowned. "Is there something wrong with my clothes?"

"You'll want to wear pants, but jeans are too heavy. A lighter fabric will breathe and won't absorb so much of the sun's rays. The tennis shoes aren't ideal, but I don't think you'll want to try breaking in new boots for this."

"Okay…"

"And we'll need to get you a pack."

"A pack?" she asked.

Quinn nodded. "For your water, some food, sunscreen, flashlight, emergency blanket and a first-aid kit."

"I see."

"And a hat," he added. "You'll probably want sunglasses, too."

Rebecca's expression was one of resignation. "This isn't going to be as easy as I'd hoped."

"I was a Boy Scout growing up," Quinn explained. "And what kind of park ranger would I be if I didn't insist on taking safety precautions before we set out?"

"Where can I get this stuff?" she asked on a sigh.

"I have a spare pack at home," he said. "But we'll need to head into town to get you the right pants."

"Let's go, then. I don't want to lose any more time than necessary."

Chapter 3

It didn't take long to reach the feed store. She spent the drive in the passenger seat, typing out a message to Frank, telling him of her plans to go out on the trail with Quinn. She told him she'd check in by 9:00 pm, just as a precaution. Having taken care of that, Quinn led her inside the store and pointed out the style of pants she should buy. Rebecca tried on her size and, satisfied with the result, ripped off the tag and brought it to the register.

"Might as well wear them out," she said. She grabbed a second pair and looked at Quinn. "What else do I need?"

He picked up a wide-brimmed hat and set it on top of the pants. "This'll do. I have everything else."

She paid for everything and they returned to the car. "My apartment isn't far," he said quietly.

He directed her to a small complex near the edge of the town and led her up a flight of stairs to a door on the second floor. Rebecca glanced around, surprised at the beauty of the view. "You can see the mountains from here," she remarked.

Quinn glanced behind him as he unlocked the door. "Yeah. It's especially pretty at sunrise and sunset."

He walked inside, holding the door so she could follow. She stepped into the living room and saw the kitchen off to the right. A short hall extended to the left, where she assumed his bedroom was.

"Bathroom is just that way," he said, indicating the hall with a nod. "If you need it."

She didn't, but it gave her an excuse to snoop. "Thanks." She headed down the hall as he opened a closet door in the living room and began to rummage inside. Satisfied he was occupied, she risked a quick glance into his bedroom. Nothing fancy; she noted a bed and a side table sporting a lamp and a framed picture.

His wife, she guessed. It was too far away for her to make out the image, but who else would it be?

She ducked into the bathroom, which was small but clean. She reached for the mirrored cabinet hanging on the wall, then hesitated. It felt wrong to invade Quinn's privacy by snooping in his medicine cabinet, but she needed to know if he was taking anything that might make him an unreliable source. Pushing aside the hint of guilt, she opened the cabinet and was greeted with the sight of nothing special. His toothbrush, toothpaste and razor were there, along with a few bottles of ibuprofen and an over-the-counter allergy medication. Certainly nothing that suggested drug abuse, or any physical or mental health issues. It was possible he kept medication in his bedside table drawer, but from what she saw here, Quinn appeared to be a healthy man. It all fit with the results of his background check—by all reports, Quinn was a law-abiding guy who had never been in trouble with the authorities.

She quietly closed the cabinet, then flushed the toilet and ran the faucet to make it sound like she'd used the facilities. She stepped back into the hall and headed for the living room to find Quinn sitting on the floor, two backpacks in front of him. He had opened one and was methodically going through the supplies, apparently double-checking the contents against a mental list.

"Mind if I get something to drink?"

He shook his head, not bothering to look up. "There's bottled water in the fridge. Grab me one, too, please. We need to start hydrating before we set out."

Rebecca headed into the kitchen, noting it was just as tidy as the bathroom. No dishes cluttered the sink, and aside from a coffee maker, the counters were bare. She opened the fridge, half-expecting it to be empty. But it was stocked with a variety of fruits and vegetables, along with a gallon of milk, some juice and a few condiments. There was a full six-pack of beer shoved to the back of the shelf, which told her Quinn wasn't much of a drinker. She found the water and grabbed two bottles, then headed back into the living room.

Quinn was packing up the first bag and as she walked over, he zipped it closed and reached for the second pack. He hesitated a brief second, then opened it and began the inventory process again.

"Everything okay?" she asked. She settled onto the rug across from him and took a sip of water. She felt her eyes grow wide as he pulled an impressive assortment of gear from the small bag.

"Yep." He cracked open his own water bottle and took a healthy drink. "Just double-checking every-thing before we set out."

"Do we really need all this stuff?" There were ropes, a flashlight, a small pill bottle containing cot-ton and a few matches, a first-aid kit, some kind of strange-looking tube, a small shiny square wrapped in plastic and many more items she didn't recognize. She reached for the flashlight, flicking it on. "We're not going to be out at night."

Quinn reached over and took the light, turning it off before setting it back on the floor. "You never know," he said. "Better to have it and not need it than the opposite. I've seen too many hikers get into trou-ble because they thought they could skimp on safety."

"Fair enough." She wouldn't ask a fellow agent to

go into a raid without a bulletproof vest, and the feel of her ankle holster was a reminder she'd made her own preparations for this hike. She couldn't really blame Quinn for doing his job properly.

Even though it meant her back would ache the whole trip.

"It's not as heavy as you think," Quinn said, apparently reading her mind. "If you pack it properly so the weight is evenly distributed, it's not that bad. The heaviest thing you'll be carrying is water, and that will get lighter as we go."

"If you say so," she said, unable to keep a note of doubt from her voice. Given the amount of gear Quinn was shoving back into the bag, Rebecca didn't see how that was possible. But he sounded confident, so she decided to give him the benefit of the doubt.

For now.

She watched him inspect each item, then place it back into the bag. He worked quickly but competently, and Rebecca was surprised to find she enjoyed seeing him work. His hands sported a warm golden tan from time spent outside, and there was a light dusting of hair on his wrists. His long fingers moved nimbly, and she was suddenly struck with a curious desire to know how his hands would feel on her skin. The errant thought sent a burst of warmth through her limbs, and she shifted, trying to ignore the feeling.

It's just a physical reaction, that's all, she told herself. As she'd noticed during their first meeting, Quinn was a handsome man. It was only natural her body would respond in kind. But that didn't mean she was going to act on this attraction. A shiver went down her spine as the faces of the two victims flashed in her mind. Both women had been redheads, just like her. And just like Quinn's wife. How would he respond once they got out on the trail? His reaction would tell her a lot about his connection to these murders.

But even if Quinn hadn't been tied to the investigation, she wasn't ready for a relationship again. She'd tried to date a few months ago, figuring that by a year after Brandon's murder she should make some kind of effort to connect with a man. But her heart hadn't really been in it, and her efforts had stalled after a few lackluster dinners. Rebecca didn't want to spend the rest of her life alone, but she wasn't about to force herself into a relationship just so she could check that box.

Quinn got to his feet and she rose as well. He handed her the smaller backpack and she slipped it over her shoulders, surprised to find he was right—it wasn't too heavy.

"Wow," she said, tugging a bit on the straps to adjust the fit. "It really isn't that bad."

A corner of his mouth lifted in a crooked smile. "Is this where I get to say 'told you so'?"

"If you must," she replied, smiling a little.

He stepped to the side, checking how the bag sat on her back. When he faced her again, his eyes burned with a naked longing that nearly stole her breath. Then he blinked and the emotion was gone, snuffed out like a candle.

Rebecca swallowed, unsure of what to say to break the silence between them. Quinn studied her face, as if comparing her features to a memory. Rebecca bore his scrutiny silently, part of her not wanting to interrupt this strange moment. There was an undercurrent of sexual tension between them, but there was something else, too, something she couldn't quite identify buzzing under the surface. How long would this last? How would it be resolved?

Finally, Quinn bent and picked up the larger bag, slipping it onto his back. His movement broke the spell, and Rebecca let out her breath in a quiet sigh. "How long do you think this hike will take?"

He shrugged. "It's about seven miles, round-trip. A few hours at least, depending on our pace." He slipped into the kitchen and returned a few seconds later, his arms laden with more water bottles. "Here, let me get you loaded up."

She turned away from him, offering him access to the bag. The pack grew heavier as he inserted the water bottles, but it was still bearable.

"Want me to put yours in?"

Quinn shook his head. "That's okay. I've got it." He slipped off the bag and added the water. "Ready?" A flash of sadness crossed his features, and Rebecca realized with a jolt that she must be wearing his dead wife's bag. They must have gone through these preparations countless times before setting off together;

no wonder Quinn seemed a little off. Seeing another woman wear his wife's gear must be difficult for him. Rebecca could only imagine how she'd feel if she saw someone wearing Brandon's jacket or favorite tie.

She swallowed hard, her mouth dry. "Quinn, take me back to the feed store. I can buy my own bag." She didn't want to torture the man, for God's sake.

He shook his head with a small, sad smile. "It's okay. Really," he added, after seeing her face. "That's silly for you to spend money on something you'll never use again. Besides, Ashley would be glad to know her gear is getting used."

"Are you sure?"

"I am."

Rebecca reached out and placed her hand on his forearm, wanting to comfort him in some small way. "I'll be careful with it," she promised. It humbled her to know he was entrusting her with this memento of his wife. She wasn't sure she'd be able to do the same with something that had belonged to Brandon.

"I know." He jerked up one shoulder and emitted a short laugh. "I trust you. I don't know why, but I do."

Rebecca swallowed. "I'll earn it," she promised. She wanted him to know she understood the magnitude of his gesture, knew how hard this must be for him. "My fiancé was murdered almost two years ago," she blurted, the words tumbling out before she could think better of it.

Quinn's eyes widened and his mouth softened. "My God," he said softly. "I'm so sorry to hear that."

She shook her head, tears pricking her eyes. "It's okay. I just wanted you to know I get it—I know how hard it is to lose someone. And you're stronger than I am. I don't think I could let someone else use Brandon's things. Not yet."

Quinn hesitated, then reached out to pull her close. Rebecca didn't resist, and some small part of her brain was shocked at how willingly she moved into his arms. He held her in a loose hug, his broad chest warm against her cheek.

"Grief is a funny thing," he said quietly. "And I still have bad days, believe me."

She sniffed and nodded and he released her. She took a quick swipe at her eyes and tried for a smile. "Ready?" If Quinn kept looking at her like that, his eyes full of warm sympathy and understanding, she was liable to throw herself back into his arms and beg him to hold her again. His touch had been comforting, despite the fact they were practically strangers. There was something about making contact with a man who had no ulterior motive that soothed her heart and made her feel safe.

It was a revelation, and now that Rebecca knew what it felt like to be held by Quinn, she was going to have a hard time not thinking about it. She knew she was taking a risk, setting off on a remote hike with a man who was somehow tied to these murders. But there was no better way to test him than to take him back to the scene of the crime. His reaction, or lack thereof, would tell her everything she needed to know.

"Let's go," he said, apparently sensing her need to change the subject. "Do you need to pick up anything from your room before we set out? A camera or anything like that?"

Rebecca shook her head. "I've got my phone if I need to take pictures. I mostly just want to get a feel for the place, if that makes any sense."

He nodded. "It does," he said shortly. He sounded apprehensive, and she figured he wasn't looking forward to going back to the site. It was a normal reaction for a civilian to have, but she forced herself to consider another possibility: did Quinn want to avoid the area because he was afraid his reaction might give something away? She believed he wasn't the killer, but she still wasn't convinced he didn't know the murderer somehow. And if the two men were working together to choose victims, or even stage the bodies, it was possible Quinn's excitement would bleed through his innocent facade and give him away.

Rebecca glanced down, making sure her ankle holster was sufficiently hidden by the flare of her pant leg. As far as she knew, Quinn had no idea she was armed. She intended to keep it that way.

"After you," she said.

He let her set the pace, shortening his stride so he didn't push her to go too fast. It was clear Rebecca wasn't an experienced hiker, but she was in good shape, which worked to her advantage. They made decent time, despite the increasingly rugged terrain.

Seeing Rebecca wearing Ashley's gear had thrown him more than he cared to admit. It shouldn't have—it was just a backpack, for crying out loud. But seeing the familiar green bag bobbing ahead of him on the trail made it far too easy to remember all the times he and Ashley had set off to explore the trails together.

It didn't help that he felt drawn to Rebecca, either. She wasn't Ashley—his mind and body knew that. Rebecca had Ashley's red hair, but that was about it. Still, there was something about Rebecca that intrigued him and made him want to know more. At first glance, she was a walking paradox—a delicate-looking woman who spent her days staring down serial killers and other psychos. He knew better than to trust a first impression, though. In the short time he'd known her, he'd seen that Rebecca had a core of steel. She was much tougher than she looked, and he guessed she probably used her appearance to her advantage.

What other tricks did she have up her sleeve? The urge to learn about a woman was unfamiliar and he wasn't quite sure what to do with the feelings. Ignore them and hope they went away? Or indulge his curiosity in the hopes his interest would wane the way it normally did?

Time enough to decide. For now, he needed to keep his eyes on the goal: get her to the site and back safely.

"Time for another water break," he announced. He

led them off the trail a few feet to the shadow of a large rock and did a quick sweep of the ground with the sole of his boot to disturb any creepy-crawlies that might be taking advantage of the shade. Rebecca waited for his nod before sitting down. She removed her pack and took out another bottle of water, her breathing slowing as she rested.

"Doing okay?" Her face was flushed with exertion from the heat, and her tank top was damp with sweat. Quinn had been religious about enforcing water breaks, but perhaps it was time for a longer rest...

"I'm fine," she said. "Just didn't expect this much of a workout."

"Some of these trails are pretty tough going," he said sympathetically. "But we didn't pick an ideal time to set out. When I take you to the first site, we'll start before dawn and that will make a difference."

She nodded and took a healthy swig from the bottle. "Is this the only trail leading to the site?"

"Yes. But it's possible he approached from a different direction."

She considered his words for a moment. "Would it be an easier trek if he went off the trail?"

Quinn shook his head. "No. Believe it or not, the trail is the best way to get there."

Rebecca pursed her lips in thought. "So whoever did this is in excellent shape."

"Do you—" Quinn hesitated, not sure he wanted to ask the question. But he needed to know, even if the answer would only add fuel to his nightmares. "Do you know if the women were killed at the site or if they were already dead when he left them there?"

Rebecca took another drink. "The coroner thinks they were killed at the site. He erased his footprints, removing all signs of struggle as well. But I have to believe someone would have noticed a man carrying a dead body over his shoulder, even if they only saw him from far away."

"So he lured them here." The idea put a bad taste in his mouth that the water did nothing to erase. What kind of man did something so horrible? How could one human deliberately gain another's trust, knowing they intended to kill them later?

"Looks that way," she confirmed.

"Those poor women," he muttered, shaking his head. Discovering the bodies had been bad enough, but knowing the women had been led to their deaths somehow made it worse. The killer and his victim had probably traversed this same trail, chatting as they walked, perhaps stopping to admire a bird or pretty flower. Had she smiled at him, thinking him a friend? Had he shared food with her along the way?

Quinn's stomach lurched, the water no longer refreshing. He set aside the bottle and focused on a nearby cactus, trying to steer his thoughts in a different direction.

"It was quick," Rebecca offered. He glanced over to find her watching him, her gaze knowing. "He broke their necks, likely while they were resting. No signs of sexual trauma, either, so they didn't suffer that way before they died."

"Is that supposed to make it okay?" He didn't mean to sound so harsh—she was only trying to make him feel better.

"No," she said quietly. "But in my line of work, I look for the small mercies to keep me going."

"How do you do it?" He shook his head, trying to cast off his bad mood. "How can you stand to work with such evil day in and day out?" She didn't look like an adrenaline junkie, nor the type to get her rocks off on the suffering of others. But there had to be some reason she'd devoted her career to killers and criminals.

Rebecca took a drink as she pondered his question. "I don't enjoy my work—not in the sense that I think you do," she said finally. "But I derive great satisfaction from finding a killer or solving a crime. There are bad people out there, and I believe if I can understand them, even just a little bit, I can protect others. I don't want to learn about killers because they interest me—I study them so I can predict what others like them might do. I guess you could say I do this for the victims, in the hopes of preventing more deaths."

Her answer made sense, and Quinn felt his emotions settle a bit. But one question still lingered. "How do you keep from bringing your work home with you? Doesn't something like that contaminate other areas of your life?"

She shrugged. "It can, if I let it. But when I talk

to killers, I try to leave my emotions out of it. These people are predators, and it gets them off if they know they're bothering you. I refuse to give them that satisfaction. I view my job as a puzzle—I try to put the pieces in the right order to solve the case and catch the bad guy. I've gotten pretty good at building a wall between myself and what I do. I guess you could say I'm an expert at compartmentalizing things." She offered a half smile, shrugging slightly.

Quinn couldn't imagine living that way, with everything put into neat and tidy boxes that weren't allowed to touch. Maybe he was wired differently, but it seemed that every aspect of his life impacted another. It was part of why he'd loved working at Yosemite— he and Ashley had both loved hiking and camping in the park, and he'd enjoyed sharing the best parts of his job with her. The thought of working a job that needed to be set aside daily for the good of his mental health made him a little sad, and he felt a spurt of pity for Rebecca.

She doesn't need me to feel bad for her, he thought. Rebecca was clearly a thoughtful and intelligent woman who had found a career that interested her, if nothing else. She was qualified to do any number of jobs, so if she was really bothered by her career, she could find another. Just because Quinn couldn't imagine living that way didn't mean she was miserable.

Still, curiosity nagged him. Before he could think better of it, he spoke again. "Does that make it hard to have friends?"

She blinked, clearly taken aback by the question. "What, you mean my tendency to compartmentalize?" At his nod, she shook her head. "Not really. I don't talk about my work with my friends, and they know better than to ask except in the broadest of terms. Most people don't want to know the details of a serial killer's crimes, and I won't talk about those things if I think someone is just looking for a cheap thrill."

He nodded, grabbing his water for another sip. Rebecca cocked her head to the side, studying him. "What's with the twenty questions?" She sounded curious and a little bit wary, as if she hadn't decided what to make of his interest in her life.

Quinn shrugged. "You're the first FBI profiler I've met. What you do is so foreign to me—I can't imagine working with killers and investigating murder cases all the time. I'm just trying to understand how you do it, how you handle the more difficult parts." He shook his head. "I could never do that."

"You might be surprised what you can handle when you have to," she said cryptically. She recapped her bottle and glanced at her watch. "Should we get back to it?"

"Yeah." Quinn stashed his empty bottle and re-shouldered his pack. "We're not too far. Maybe another half hour?"

She waited for him to take the lead again and fell into step behind him. The rest of the hike passed in silence; it was hot, and the going was strenuous. Finally, they arrived.

It wasn't difficult to find—yellow crime-scene tape was still strung across small bushes, acting as a flimsy barrier to keep out trespassers. The ground was littered with footprints, both human and animal; he saw the distinctive mark of a mountain lion, along with what looked like prints from both a mule deer and a raccoon.

Quinn forced himself to look at the spot where he'd found the woman. He half expected to see the outline of her body in the dirt, but it was blessedly clear of marks, as the wind, animals and the police would have brushed them away. He swallowed hard and looked away to find Rebecca watching him intently.

"You okay?"

He nodded. "Yeah. I'm just…" He trailed off, rubbing a hand over his breastbone to ease the sudden ache in his chest. "I'm going to sit over here, if you don't mind. Take your time." He walked a few feet away to a large rock on the edge of the trail and sat, leaving Rebecca free to study the area to her heart's content.

Even though the site was free from any reminders of his discovery, Quinn's mind had no problem picturing the woman on the ground, her hair strewn across her face. *Not again* had been his first thought when he'd stumbled across the second body. Initially, he'd thought he was seeing things. He'd been thinking of the first victim as he'd walked, unable to get her out of his head. So when he'd come across the second woman he'd assumed he was simply having a very vivid hallucination brought on by emotional distress and the heat. But then the smell of death had hit him, and he'd realized the sight in front of him was very real.

Why me? he thought for what must have been the millionth time. Why had he been the one to find both victims? Was it simply an awful coincidence, or was there something more sinister at work?

After what seemed like an eternity, Rebecca walked over. "I'm ready."

"Did you get what you needed?" He rose to his feet, glad she was done. Maybe someday he'd be able to hike this trail without being assaulted by the memories of his gruesome discovery, but not today.

"More or less." She was quiet for a moment, the crunch of their footsteps the only sound. "I appreciate you bringing me here," she said. "I can see it was hard for you."

Quinn jerked up one shoulder in a shrug, trying to appear nonchalant. "I'm just glad you got the information you were searching for."

"I did," she murmured. "In more ways than one." He shot her a quizzical look and she shook her head. "He's physically fit, that much is obvious. Probably a frequent visitor to the park—I'm willing to bet he had this spot picked out for a while. It wasn't a spur-of-the-moment thing. He probably fantasized about bringing a woman here to kill her."

A wave of revulsion hit Quinn and he bit his lip to keep from vomiting. "We can check visitor logs at all the ranger stations," he said, his voice coming out a little hoarse. "But there's no guarantee he registered with us."

"Have the police already started combing through camping permits?"

He nodded. "Yes. But not everyone follows the rules."

"True." She sounded thoughtful. "And a man who was so careful to scrub the site probably wouldn't make the mistake of applying for a camping permit."

"You're sure it's a man?"

She tilted her head to the side. "Statistically speaking, yes. Most serial killers are men. And the women were strangled to death, which takes brute strength."

Quinn digested her words, nodding as he realized she was likely right.

"You think he's staying in the park?" The thought sent a chill down Quinn's spine. If the killer was camping in the backcountry, they might never find him. It would be like searching for a needle in a haystack.

"Anything is possible," Rebecca said. "I want to focus on the victims first, though. If they had a permit, we can try to retrace their steps in the days leading up to their deaths. If we're really lucky, we'll find a shared location or some other point where they may have crossed paths with the killer."

"You think he met them here?"

"More than likely. It's possible the first victim came with him, but the second one was definitely someone he picked up recently. And given the identical display of the bodies, I don't think he knew the women on more than a superficial level."

Quinn's curiosity got the better of him. "How can you tell that?"

"When a killer really knows his victim, he usually treats the body differently. Some murderers are overcome with guilt and treat the body almost tenderly, while some have a surge of anger and do further damage to the remains. Either way, there is usually a sign that the crime was personal. But in the case of our two victims, the bodies were staged identically. That makes me think he didn't know either one of them on an intimate level."

"He must be pretty charismatic," Quinn mused.

Rebecca's gaze sharpened. "What makes you say that?"

"He got two women—strangers, you think—to trust him enough to set off on a strenuous hike alone with him," he pointed out. "Most hikers and campers are friendly, but they're also savvy about safety. If a man I didn't know approached me and wanted to take on a remote trail together, I wouldn't go. And I'm a fairly big guy."

"Very good," she said softly. "I'm impressed you picked up on that. We'll make a profiler out of you yet, Quinn."

He blushed but didn't reply.

"There's just one thing that bothers me about this," she said.

"Only one?" Quinn joked lamely.

Rebecca acknowledged his point with a nod. "Why haven't we heard from anyone who knows the victims? These women didn't pop out of thin air. They had families, friends. Why has no one reported them missing? You just said hikers are savvy about safety, so it's unlikely they came to the park alone. Someone should have noticed when they didn't return."

"Maybe he's not meeting them in the park," Quinn said. "What if he's bringing them in from one of the neighboring towns?"

"Good point," she said. "Sounds like I need to widen my search."

"I'll go with you," he said impulsively. Rebecca raised one eyebrow in surprise. "The people in these little towns aren't always welcoming to outsiders. I'm not going to get in your way, but I don't think you should go by yourself." He didn't like the thought of her going off alone, especially not with a murderer on the loose. As an FBI agent she'd probably had self-defense training, but she still could be overpowered by the brute strength of a determined assailant. Quinn didn't have any illusions regarding his fighting prowess, but he was on the larger side and knew how to throw a punch.

When Rebecca didn't reply, he added, "If you don't want me to tag along, at least take a police officer with you."

"That won't be necessary," she replied. A smile tugged at the corners of her mouth. "I think you'll do just fine."

Chapter 4

The sun was low in the sky by the time they got back to the trailhead. Rebecca was sweaty, dusty, flushed with heat and thoroughly tired. But it had been worth it. Seeing the site had confirmed some of her first impressions regarding the killer, and watching Quinn's reactions made her even more confident he wasn't involved in these deaths.

He hadn't said much during the hike back, and she was fine with the silence. It gave her space to think, to try to organize her thoughts and plan her next steps. She needed to talk to the police, find out what progress they'd made in tracking the victims. They were still searching for the names of the women, but hopefully a friend or relative would step forward soon with information. The coroner's initial physical examination had revealed the victims were in good shape and didn't show signs of being runaways or of having lived rough recently. Someone should be missing them... Maybe it was time to blast the national news with their pictures and widen the search.

"Do you—" Quinn began, then stopped abruptly, shaking his head.

"Do I what?"

He bit his bottom lip, hesitating. Then with a small shrug, he spoke again. "I just can't figure out why *I* discovered both women. There are dozens of people who work here and are out and about every day, in every area of the park. I wouldn't want anyone to find what I did, but I don't understand why I had to be the one to come across both victims." There was a hint of anguish in his voice, and Rebecca could tell he'd been haunted by the question probably since he'd found the first body.

"That is unusual," she said. "And it makes me wonder if the placement of the bodies wasn't random."

His face went pale under the brim of his hat. "You think the killer meant for me to find them?"

"I think we need to consider that possibility, yes."

"But...why? And how would he do that?"

Rebecca tilted her head to the side. "The *why* is harder to answer, at least right now. As to the *how*, I'm assuming you have a daily routine? Certain trails you check frequently, or specific areas of the park that you cover?"

Quinn nodded, looking gobsmacked. "Yes. I lead guided tours on some of the trails, and when I found the first woman, I'd been sent to check on a section of fencing at the top of the mountain that some hikers had reported was damaged."

"And was it?" That was a hell of a coincidence. Was one of the hikers the killer, creating a false report of damage to deliberately lead Quinn to the first victim?

"I—I don't know," he admitted. "I stopped when I found her, and after the police arrived I didn't think to go on and check the fencing."

"Hmmm," she mused. "Who talked to the hikers?"

"I'm not sure who was on duty at the front desk that day. We can check the logs." By this time they had reached the parking lot of the ranger station. Quinn's revelation put a burst of energy into Rebecca's step and she picked up the pace, her earlier fatigue forgotten.

Quinn caught up with her and held open the door, then led her through the lobby into a room of cubicles. He sat at a desk and gestured for her to take the chair across from him. She perched on the edge, watching as his fingers danced across the keyboard. "Looks like Sam Oberlin was on duty that morning," he said.

"Is he here now?" Rebecca scanned the room, noting with disappointment only two other people were still working.

Quinn shook his head. "He works the early morning shift. You can talk to him tomorrow."

"What's the procedure when a visitor reports damage like that? Do you get a name and contact information?" *Please, please, please*, she thought. If one of the hikers was the killer, he probably hadn't left his real name. But it wouldn't take long to discover he'd been lying, and she'd at least have a description of the man's face and body to help narrow the search.

"Sometimes," Quinn replied. "But usually we just take the information and check it out."

Rebecca pressed her lips together, trying to suppress the frustration welling in her chest. "Okay," she said. "I still need to talk to Sam, though. Maybe he remembers what the men looked like, or got their names even if he didn't record them."

"I hope so," Quinn said. He sounded disappointed as well, as if he'd hoped to be able to deliver better news. "Do you still want to hike to the first site tomorrow? We'll need to start early if you do."

Rebecca considered his question for a moment. Would she learn anything new by seeing the first spot in person? Or would her time be better served combing through the small towns dotting the area outside the park in the hopes of finding more information on the victims?

"What do you think?" she asked, curious to see his reaction. He'd struggled with their return to the second dump site today. Would he try to talk her out of going to the first one?

"It's your show," he said, his expression impassive. "I'll do whatever you need to help the investigation. I will warn you, though—the hike up the mountain is more difficult than the one we took today. If you do want to go, it might be a good idea to rest a day or two before we try to tackle it, since you're not used to hiking."

Rebecca nodded. "That sounds reasonable. In the meantime, I want to start checking out the nearby towns. Maybe one of the victims passed through on her way to the park."

"What time do you want to get started?"

She appreciated his ready offer of help, and despite her resolve to keep her distance from him, her respect for him grew. "Early. We'll talk to Sam first and go from there." She rose from the chair and Quinn stood as well, an automatic display of manners that she'd come to realize was ingrained in him.

"Sounds good. I'll meet you here." He rounded his desk, and she realized he intended to walk her to her car. The gesture made her feel feminine in a way she hadn't in a long time, and she decided to enjoy it.

"Thanks for today," she said as they walked out of the building. "I know it was hard for you."

He acknowledged her words with a nod. "I'm just glad it helped you." His voice was deep and quiet in the gloaming, and for a moment Rebecca felt like they were the only two people in the park.

They arrived at her car and she stood by the door, suddenly reluctant to leave. What was it about this man that made her feel comfortable in his company? She had to be careful; if she didn't watch herself, she'd let down her guard and start to trust him.

"Make sure you keep drinking water tonight," he

said. There was nothing personal about his words, but the advice felt intimate somehow, the expression of concern something a friend might say.

Or a lover.

A shiver shot through Rebecca's limbs and she nodded, not trusting her voice.

"Drive safely." His mouth curved up in a small smile, and she realized with a jolt he was waiting for her to get into the car and leave.

Smooth, she thought to herself. *Real smooth.* "You, too," she said. She climbed behind the wheel. "Good night."

Quinn stayed in the parking lot as she drove away, watching her leave with an expression she couldn't identify. Was she the only one affected by these odd moments, or did he feel the frissons, too?

"It doesn't matter," she muttered as she turned on to the main road that led out of the park. She had one job: solve these murders. Then she could go home, back to her normal, comfortable routine and far away from handsome park rangers who stirred her emotions.

The thought should have brought relief. Instead, a vague sense of dissatisfaction settled over her as she drove away from the park. And Quinn.

Quinn loaded the backpacks into the trunk of his car, his thoughts on Rebecca and the day they'd spent together. He'd finally figured out why he found her so appealing—her mind fascinated him. There was something deeply satisfying about watching her think, seeing the way she worked through a problem or an issue. He'd been distracted by bad memories at the site, but he'd still caught glimpses of the way she'd moved around the area, stooping here, crouching there, even climbing up on rocks to change her vantage point. He'd figured after all the photos and evidence collected by the police there wouldn't be much in the way for her to find, but apparently she had a different approach.

It seemed to work for her. She'd appeared satisfied as they'd set off for home again. He was glad to have been useful, even indirectly. Leading her to the site had helped relieve the awful sense of helplessness that had plagued him since discovering the first woman. He'd arrived too late to save the first two victims, but hopefully by helping Rebecca he could play a role in stopping the killer before he hurt anyone else.

He slid behind the wheel of the car, his thoughts turning to their conversation along the way. Her ability to compartmentalize things was something he both envied and found totally foreign. Did she put every aspect of her life into a neat little box, or were some things too big, too messy, to pack away like winter clothes? What would it take to break through her emotional insulation, to really reach her soul?

Suddenly, he recalled the feel of her body against his own, her curves pressed to his chest as he'd hugged her. Heat suffused his limbs and his skin tingled at the sense memory. A small tendril of shame sprouted at his body's response. There had been nothing sexual about the embrace—he'd simply been offering comfort in the wake of her admission about her fiancé. It didn't seem right for him to appreciate the contact on any kind of physical level. But his hormones didn't care. He hadn't deliberately embraced a woman in a long time, and the memory of this hug wasn't going to fade soon.

Quinn shouldn't have touched her. But she'd looked so lost, standing in front of him with tears welling in her eyes. Her admission had shocked him and she'd looked just as surprised, as if she couldn't believe she'd actually told him something so personal. He'd felt the need to do *something* to help her, so he'd acted on instinct and pulled her into his arms. Now he was paying the price for his mistake.

Of all the times for him to start to *feel* again… He shook his head as he navigated the dark road toward home. His libido had picked a hell of a time to wake up. Rebecca was here to track a killer, and it was his job to help her in any way he could. Attraction had no place in the equation, and he needed to remember it.

"Can I buy you a drink?"

The woman turned to face him, the motion nearly sending her off the bar stool. "Whoops," she giggled, her breath a blast of alcoholic fumes that made his eyes water. "Hi there, s-stranger," she said, slurring.

He smiled, eyeing her up and down. He'd been watching her from across the bar; she'd started out with a group of friends, but as the hour had grown late, the women had left one by one until she was alone. Her friends had tried to convince her to leave, too, but she'd brushed off their concern. It was plain to everyone she had eyes for the bartender—she was clearly hoping that staying until closing time would result in the offer of a ride home.

"What's your name?" he asked.

Her smile grew wider and she shot the bartender a quick look to see if he had noticed her new suitor. The other man was at the other end of the bar, taking an order. He was paying no attention to the woman, and for a second her lips turned down in a pout. Then she gathered herself and focused on him again.

"What do you want it to be?" she said, trying to sound coy.

"Hmmm…" He pretended to think as he reached out to brush a strand of hair behind her ear. It was dark, almost purplish-red, not really the right color at all. But it would do for now. "You look like a Crystal to me."

Her eyes widened. "Wow, you're good." Little did she know he'd overheard her friends talking to her earlier. For a split second, he felt a spurt of pity for the woman. She was making it too easy for him—there was little satisfaction in bringing down such easy prey. But it was time to leave Quinn Gallagher another gift, and she was his best prospect right now, so…

"Are you waiting for someone?"

She cast another quick glance at the bartender. The other man was still pointedly ignoring her, apparently not wanting to offer any encouragement. She pursed her lips and turned back. "I was, but not anymore."

His smile was genuine. "I'm glad to hear it. Wanna get out of here?"

Crystal started to nod, then paused. "Maybe. What's your name?"

"John," he responded, lying easily. "I'm in town to do some hiking in Big Bend. It'd be nice to have some company…" He trailed off, the suggestion clear.

Crystal leaned forward, thrusting her breasts out as she trailed a finger down his arm. "Is that all you want to do?"

He dipped his head and nipped at her bottom lip, his hand sliding up her outer thigh. "I can think of other ways to pass the time."

She hopped off the bar stool, grabbing his shoulders for support as she swayed unsteadily on her heels. "My place," she declared. "It's not far. And my bed is nicer than anything in a hotel."

"Sounds good," he agreed. He led her into the parking lot, steering her toward the rental car he'd picked up that morning. He'd been careful to switch cars between victims to ensure there was no evidence left in the vehicle he was driving. He was just getting started, and he didn't want a silly thing like a strand of hair left behind on a seat cushion to be his undoing.

He poured Crystal into the passenger seat, half-expecting her to pass out on the drive. But she stayed awake and gave surprisingly lucid directions to her apartment complex, which turned out to be close to the bar. She climbed out of the car and led him up a set of stairs, stumbling only a little as she dug in her purse for keys. She dropped them on the mat and bent at the waist, flashing him a view of the pink panties she wore under her short skirt. He couldn't decide if the action was a deliberate attempt at seduction, or if she was too drunk to know what she was doing.

He had his answer a moment later. She tugged him into the apartment and shut the door, then pushed him up against it and began fumbling at his belt as her mouth found his. He tolerated the attention; he hadn't actually intended to sleep with her tonight. The plan was to make her think they'd had sex, then convince her to go hiking with him in the morning. But Crystal was determined, and she unfastened his pants with a practiced ease that made it clear she was no stranger to one-night stands. A jolt went through him as she worked her hand, and against his better judgment, he felt himself respond to her touch.

She tore her mouth free, her chest heaving as her breath came fast and hard. "Bedroom is this way." She set off down the hall, still gripping him. He had no choice but to follow as she led him into a small room strewn with clothes and discarded shoes. Crystal wasted no time stripping down, her shirt and skirt hitting the ground, followed quickly by her bra and panties.

She was a beautiful woman, he could say that objectively. Full-figured and uninhibited, she was every man's fantasy. *Why not?* he thought to himself. He might as well enjoy himself while he was here.

"Condoms?" No way was he going to risk leaving any evidence behind. Crystal didn't know it, but she had a date with the morgue tomorrow. He was happy to show her a good time tonight, but not at the risk of his own freedom.

She crawled across the mattress, reaching for the drawer of her bedside table. She rummaged inside for a second, then turned back with a long strip of foil packets dangling from her fingertips. "Up for a challenge?"

He smiled and joined her on the bed. "Let's find out."

Chapter 5

The morning was clear and bright, the sun sitting high in the sky with no hint of clouds. It was bound to be a scorcher in the afternoon, but for now a light breeze kept the worst of the heat at bay. Rebecca grabbed her water bottle—she'd taken Quinn's advice to heart last night—and climbed out of the car.

Yesterday had been informative, to say the least. Walking around the site itself had been helpful, but not nearly as much as spending time with Quinn and cataloging his reactions. The more she knew about the man, the more convinced she became that he wasn't the killer or involved with him. If anything, he seemed to be yet another victim in this whole mess.

Why was I the one who found them? His question had dogged her all evening, running through her mind on a continuous loop. It was something she wanted to know herself. Whoever had killed those women had meant for Quinn to find the bodies. But the killer hadn't left behind any evidence to try to frame Quinn for the murders. If the murderer intended to frame Quinn, he was probably planning to kill again so he could stage the scene and possibly leave something of Quinn's behind. Should she warn him to be extra careful with his personal effects? Or would that only serve to make him even more stressed about the situation? Was the killer simply trying to torture Quinn? Or was he working his way up to implicating Quinn in the deaths? The possibility sent a chill down her spine.

One thing was for certain—the killer had a personal connection to the ranger, even if he was only trying to send a message.

She headed for the entrance to the ranger station, hoping that Quinn's co-worker Sam might be able to shed some light on the investigation. It was probably too much to hope for that the killer had been one of the hikers who'd reported the damage to the fence, but everyone made mistakes…

She walked inside, the blast of cool air making goose bumps pop out on her arms. The young woman behind the desk smiled in recognition and waved her back. "Quinn's expecting you," she said.

Rebecca thanked her and walked past the desk, headed for the room beyond. She paused before entering and took a deep breath. Would she still feel that strange pull toward him today? Or had yesterday's emotions simply been a result of too much physical exertion in the heat?

Quinn was standing with his back toward her, studying the large whiteboard mounted on the wall. Even from this distance she felt a tug, as if someone had tied a rope around her waist and was now gently but insistently pulling her forward.

This isn't smart, she told herself as she approached him. But telling herself not to feel was like trying to control the weather—it simply wasn't going to happen. So rather than fight this strange attraction, she let it wash over her. Just because she was drawn to Quinn didn't mean she had to act on her feelings. She could still control her behavior, at least.

"Morning," she said.

He turned and flashed a smile. "Hey there." His voice was a little raspy this early in the morning, and the sound danced along her skin like a caress. He took a sip of coffee. "How'd you sleep?"

"Like the dead," she said, then winced. "Sorry, poor choice of words."

He chuckled softly. "That's okay. I know what you meant. I figured you might be tired from the hike yesterday. Have you been drinking water?"

Rebecca held up her bottle, touched at his concern. "I did take your advice."

Quinn nodded approvingly. "Glad to hear it. The last thing you want is to get dehydrated out here."

"Does that happen a lot?"

He tilted his head to the side. "It's not uncommon for people to pack too lightly when it comes to water. It's a heavy thing to carry, and a lot of times people underestimate the amount they need to drink."

"How difficult is it to get a medical evacuation in the park?" It was a question she should have considered yesterday, but she'd assumed that hiking with Quinn would keep her safe.

"Depends on the location," he said with a shrug. "But we can't just snap our fingers and get help. It takes a while, even under good conditions."

She nodded, mulling over his response. Yesterday's hike had been strenuous, but she hadn't felt alone, probably because she'd been with Quinn. Now she realized just how remote the landscape was, how it could be possible for a person to walk for miles and never encounter anyone else. It was probably another reason the killer had chosen this location.

A swell of pity rose in her chest for the women he'd murdered. They'd never stood a chance. Even if they had known what was coming and tried to fight back, they would have been alone in an unforgiving land, probably injured, with no way of contacting anyone for help. Had they screamed at the end, even knowing it was useless to do so?

"Hey." Quinn touched her arm, drawing her out of her thoughts. She blinked up at him. "Where'd you go?" he asked. "You got a funny look on your face for a minute."

Rebecca shook her head. "Sorry. I was just thinking about the case. How the fates of the women were sealed as soon as they set off with the killer."

A shadow crossed Quinn's face. "Yeah," he said quietly. "That's the bit that upsets me the most. He probably walked with them the whole time pretending everything was normal, but he knew he was going to kill them. I don't understand how someone could do that."

"Most people like to think that serial killers are pure evil, that they're not really human. Members of the public feel better if they can find a way to separate themselves from these murderers. But like it or not, we have more in common with these guys than we care to admit."

"Maybe so," Quinn said doubtfully. "But I still don't want to know how his mind works."

"You don't need to," Rebecca assured him. "That's my job."

Quinn nodded. "Speaking of jobs, I think I just heard Sam come in. Are you ready to talk to him?"

"Yes." Anticipation sparked to life in her belly. She glanced around the room, searching for a new face. "Where is he?"

"Whoa there," Quinn said with a laugh. "Let's give the man a chance to get a cup of coffee first before you bombard him with questions."

Rebecca made a face but waited while a white-haired man ambled over to the coffeepot. He seemed to have only one speed—glacial.

Apparently, Quinn sensed her impatience. He leaned close to whisper in her ear. "Sam's been a ranger at Big Bend for almost thirty years. I know he doesn't look like much, but he's a pro."

Quinn's breath was warm against her skin and smelled of fresh coffee. Rebecca resisted the temptation to lean back against his chest, to feel the solid strength of him against her shoulders and back. Instead she nodded, silently acknowledging his words.

It took Sam a few minutes to fix his morning brew and settle in behind his desk. Quinn led her over and made the introductions. "Morning, Sam. Got a minute?"

Sam glanced up, smiling when he saw Quinn. "For you? Always."

"This is Rebecca Wade. She's with the FBI, and she's working on the case of the two women found in the park. She was hoping to ask you a few questions."

A shadow crossed Sam's face at the mention of the victims. "Hell of a thing," he muttered. "I'm happy to help any way I can."

Quinn dragged a couple of chairs over, gesturing for Rebecca to sit. "What do you need from me, young lady?"

"I was hoping you could tell me about the hikers who reported the damaged fence. Do you remember anything about them?"

Sam frowned, clearly trying to dredge up the memory. "That was a couple of weeks ago. Let me think…"

He was silent a moment, pondering. Rebecca's hope dwindled with each second that ticked by. It was a long shot to think the man would recall two faces out of the hundreds he encountered every week, especially because so much time had since elapsed.

"Well, now. It was two young men," he said finally. "Both lean and fit—real serious hikers. Probably about twenty-five. Maybe a little older, maybe a little younger—hard to tell, since they spent so much time outdoors."

"Is there any security footage of them coming into the station?"

Sam shook his head. "I'm afraid not. We don't keep the footage for that long—not enough storage, I'm afraid."

Rebecca tried not to let her disappointment show. "Did you happen to get their names?" She didn't hold out hope, but she had to ask...

Sam's face cleared. "Now that I did do." He pushed back from the desk. "Wait right here. I'll go get the log book."

Rebecca turned to Quinn, unable to contain a smile. She put her hand on his arm and squeezed. "Cross your fingers this pans out."

Quinn smiled back, then moved to cover her hand with his own. His palm was large and felt rough against her skin, sending a tingle of sensation up her arm. "I will," he said quietly.

Oh, no, she chided herself. *Why did I touch him?* She'd acted impulsively, driven by excitement over the possibility of a break in the investigation. But she couldn't afford to let down her guard. She was growing more comfortable around Quinn, and it would be all too easy to relax and let her emotions take the wheel. The two dead women deserved better than that.

Sam returned, his nose buried in a large spiral-bound notebook. Rebecca slipped her hand free, her skin still warm from Quinn's touch. Something flashed in Quinn's eyes—disappointment? Surely not. But there was no time for her to worry about it.

"Here we go," Sam said. He placed the notebook on his desk, facing her, his forefinger pressed on two names. "These were the kids. Used student IDs for identification, so I put down the name of their schools as well. Will that help?"

"Yes, thank you." Rebecca leaned forward, jotting down the information. "You've been a huge help. I really appreciate it."

Sam beamed up at her, his cheeks going pink. "My pleasure, young lady. You let me know if I can do anything else."

"Thanks, Sam," Quinn said. He led Rebecca back to his desk. She grabbed her phone and in a matter of minutes, had placed calls to the men's universities, asking campus police to verify their whereabouts. "Do you recognize these names?"

Quinn shook his head. "I don't. Sorry."

She puffed her cheeks as she exhaled. "Don't be. It was a long shot. Still, it's good to tie this thread off. Keeps us from wasting time chasing our tails." She logged on to an FBI database and typed in the names, running a quick search to see if either man showed up in the system. They didn't, but that only meant they hadn't had any run-ins with law enforcement. She wasn't going to exclude them as potential suspects just yet, but they didn't seem like very likely candidates for the killer.

"What would you like to do now?"

"You still up for taking me to the nearby towns? I called the local police last night—they haven't had much luck identifying the victims, and they don't have the man power to do a thorough canvas of every small town in the area."

"I'll take you wherever you want to go."

It was an incredibly generous offer, one she appreciated. "Do you need to clear the time off with your boss? I'd hate to cause trouble for you."

Quinn shook his head. "Gary's already told me to do whatever it takes to help you."

The news was welcome, but she felt an irrational stab of disappointment nonetheless. *What did you expect?* she told herself. *He's not spending time with you simply because he likes you.* She cast aside the annoying feeling, pulling up a map of the area on her phone. Half a dozen dots popped up on the screen, and that was just on the US side of the border. What about towns in Mexico? Her stomach sank as she realized the magnitude of what they were going to attempt.

"Any suggestions on where to start?"

Quinn considered the question. "I say we try Terlingua first. The place tends to attract a certain type of misfit, and since no one's come forward to claim these women, they might have been looking to disappear."

She frowned. "Isn't that just a ghost town?"

He smiled. "Oh, it's a little more than that. You'll see."

"Terlingua started out as a mining town," Quinn explained to Rebecca as the first low buildings came into view.

"Mining for what?"

"Mercury. They found it in the late 1800s, and the place was booming by the turn of the century. But the mining company went bankrupt in the 1940s, and the place turned into a ghost town soon thereafter. Now it's the base for several Big Bend tour companies, and the residents are a little…quirky." *To say the least*, he added silently. Terlingua was like no other place on earth, and the people who made it their home were simultaneously tough, independent, generous and distrusting of outsiders.

It was the last quality they'd have to overcome if they wanted to get any information about the two victims. Assuming the women had passed through here in the first place.

He pulled up to Starlight Theatre, one of the main restaurants in town. He caught Rebecca's wide eyes, and imagined seeing it for the first time. An old, rusted-out hulk of a car sat nearby, and the adobe walls of the building were weathered and cracked. The restaurant name was splayed over the doorway in what had once been bright blue paint. Now it was faded and worn, a testament to the sun and wind.

"Ready?"

She lifted one eyebrow. "I suppose so."

He held open the door and nearly walked into her back as she drew up short. "What's wrong?" he asked.

"There's a goat in here."

Quinn looked over her shoulder and laughed softly. He'd forgotten about the taxidermic specimen inside, standing proud with a bottle of beer tipped back in his mouth. "That's just Clay."

"Clay?"

"Clay Henry. He was the mayor of a small town nearby."

"The people really elected a goat?"

Quinn merely nodded. Rebecca's expression morphed from disbelief to resigned acceptance. "Right," she muttered. "As you do."

"I told you this place was quirky." He placed his hand on the small of her back and gently guided her inside. It felt so natural to touch her, like it was something he did all the time. If he wasn't careful, he could easily grow to care about Rebecca on a personal level.

But that wasn't why she was here, and he needed to remember it.

If she objected to his touch, she didn't show it.

She hung back a half step, sticking close to his side as she let him take the lead. "Bar?" he asked softly.

"Might as well," she said.

It was lunchtime, but there was no shortage of people looking for a drink. The place was busy but not overly crowded, and they had no trouble finding spots at the bar. The bartender approached after a moment. "What can I get you folks?"

"Sweet tea," Quinn replied promptly.

"Uh, same," Rebecca said.

The man ran his gaze over them both, clearly assessing them. He returned a few seconds later with their drinks. "Want food?"

"Actually—" Rebecca began. Quinn placed his hand on her knee, and her mouth snapped shut.

"You still have that loaded burger? The one with the pound of meat topped with fried eggs and pickled jalapeños?"

The bartender's shoulders relaxed a bit and the corner of his mouth quirked up. "We do. Think you can handle it?"

Quinn patted his flat stomach. "Let's find out."

The man turned to Rebecca, who looked a little lost. "The chili is good," Quinn suggested quietly. "So's the barbeque sandwich."

"I'll take the sandwich, please," she said.

The man nodded and went to punch in their orders. Quinn realized his hand was still on Rebecca's knee. He pulled it away, silently chiding himself for touching her again.

"I know you want to start asking questions, but that approach isn't going to work here," he said softly. She stiffened, and he quickly added, "I'm not trying to tell you how to do your job. But we need to ease into it if you want honest responses."

"Okay," she said simply. "I trust you."

A thrill went through him at her words. He got the impression Rebecca was a woman who didn't use that phrase casually—her trust was something that had to be earned. It meant something to know he'd proved himself worthy of her regard.

She was so different from Ashley, he mused. It wasn't fair to compare the two women, but he couldn't help it. Rebecca was the first woman he'd spent a significant amount of time with since Ashley's death, with the exception of his mother and sister. It was only natural he'd look for similarities—and differences. And while they shared some characteristics, it was clear they were very different people. Ashley had been bubbly and open, always ready to laugh. She'd never met a stranger. Rebecca was different— quiet, reserved. A much harder nut to crack. But she fascinated him nonetheless.

She looked around as they waited for their food, taking in everything about the unique place. The interior was a large rectangle, with a stage set up at the far end. A large, colorful mural on the wall behind the stage depicted a small group of campers surrounding a fire. The rest of the walls had various paintings and decorations hung on the peeling adobe. The irregular tables added to the decor—some were plain wood, while others boasted colorful scenes painted on top or tiles with a mix of pottery shards. Even though Rebecca never overtly stared at anything, Quinn got the impression she didn't miss a thing.

The bartender returned to slide plates in front of them. Rebecca's eyes widened as she caught sight of his burger. "You have *got* to be kidding me," she said.

The man grinned at Quinn. "Good luck," he said.

"Thanks," Quinn replied. "I'm going to need it."

He studied the towering monstrosity for a moment, trying to figure out the best plan of attack. The handle of a large steak knife protruded from the top bun, and he decided the best approach was probably to divide and conquer. He removed the knife, smushed down the burger as best he could, then cut it in half and took a healthy bite.

Rebecca simply stared, disbelief and amusement in her eyes. "Is this some kind of pissing contest?" she asked under her breath. "A strange male ritual I've never heard of before?"

Quinn shrugged. "Broke the ice, didn't it?" He nodded subtly at the bartender, who no longer regarded them with open suspicion.

Rebecca shook her head. "It's good of you to take one for the team," she replied. "But please try not to have a heart attack until we get back to civilization."

"Deal," he said around a mouthful.

The bartender returned a moment later with fresh drinks. "Cops or feds?" he asked casually.

Quinn pointed at his chest as he swallowed. "Park ranger." Then he jerked his thumb in Rebecca's direction. "Fed."

The man nodded. "What brings you here?" The question sounded casual, but there was a thread of wariness in his voice.

Quinn glanced at Rebecca. *Your show now.*

"Have you heard about the two women found dead in Big Bend?" she asked, taking a bite of her sandwich.

The man frowned. "Yeah. Some of the guides were in here a few days ago talking about it. A real shame."

Rebecca nodded. "It is. Even more so because we don't know their names yet. I'm hoping someone from around here might be able to help identify them."

"Got pictures?"

Quinn stiffened as Rebecca pulled two photos from her bag and placed them on the worn surface of the bar. He forced himself to look, to bear witness to these women. He braced himself for the sight of their tangled hair, their unseeing eyes.

But he needn't have worried. These photos hadn't been captured at the scene of the crime—they were portraits taken from the sterile confines of the morgue. The women looked totally different now. The hair had been combed and brushed from their faces, their skin clean, their eyes closed. There was no visible indication of how they had died. Only the paleness of their skin and the brightness of the light in the photos made it clear they were dead and not simply sleeping.

Quinn stared at the pictures, trying to erase the earlier images burned into his brain. It eased something inside him to see them look so…peaceful. Hopefully, he could remember them like this, instead of the way he'd found them.

The bartender looked at one picture and shook his head. "I don't know her," he said. Then he turned his attention to the second image, and his mouth parted. "Oh," he said dully.

Quinn felt Rebecca tense beside him, but to her credit, she didn't pounce on the man's reaction. He studied the picture a few seconds more, then glanced up. "I recognize her." He placed his fingertip on the corner of the image and tapped hesitantly, as if he was afraid to touch the picture.

"Where have you seen her before?" Rebecca asked softly.

"She came into town a few weeks ago," he said. "Tried to get a job here, but we're not hiring right now. I sent her over to Dan's place." He rattled off the name of another well-known establishment, one Quinn knew had a reputation for being much rougher around the edges. "He hired her as a waitress. Don't know where she was from. I didn't ask, and she didn't volunteer."

"What's her name?"

"Jenny," the man replied. "Not sure about a last name—Dan could probably tell you that."

Let's hope so, Quinn thought. There was no guarantee Dan had bothered to file the necessary paperwork after hiring her, but hopefully he had at least gotten her last name.

"Do you know where she was staying in town?" Rebecca asked. She had pulled out her notebook and was unobtrusively jotting down information as the bartender spoke.

"Last I heard it was over at the campground on the edge of town. I think she was staying by the school bus."

Rebecca paused. "The school bus?" she asked.

The bartender nodded. "Yeah. There's an old broken-down bus parked out there. People have incorporated it into the camp. It's by the community kitchen."

"Got it." She scribbled a bit more. "And what's your name?"

The bartender's shoulders stiffened. "You're not in any trouble," Rebecca said. "But if I have additional questions, or if the police need more information, I need to be able to tell them who I talked to."

The man frowned slightly. "Paul," he said reluctantly. "Paul Garret."

"Thanks for your help, Paul," she said. She snapped the notebook shut and returned to her sandwich. "Do you think anyone else here knew Jenny, or might possibly recognize the other woman?"

Paul shook his head. "Doubt it. I was the one Jenny

talked to when she applied for a job here. You'll have better luck at Dan's place."

"Is it far from here?"

"Nope. Just down the road a bit. There's not a big sign, but the building is half-underground. Can't miss it."

"I know the place," Quinn said.

"It doesn't open until five," Paul cautioned. "But Dan's usually there around this time getting stuff ready for the evening crew."

"Thanks," Quinn said. The man nodded and walked away, moving to the far end of the bar to check on other customers.

"This is a totally different world, isn't it?" Rebecca said softly. She watched Paul interact with the locals, a small group of men who were chatting and laughing amiably. The gang cast a few curious glances in their direction, but otherwise didn't approach.

Quinn dipped a fry in ketchup and hummed thoughtfully. "It's definitely not your usual kind of place. It has a reputation of being a town of last resort, the kind of place people land when they have nowhere else to go." He glanced around at the lunch crowd, which he suspected was mostly tourists. "I don't know how much of that is true anymore, but for a while the town seemed to cultivate an outlaw vibe." He took another bite of his burger, then set it down with a sigh.

Rebecca glanced at the remains on his plate,

amusement dancing in her eyes. "Throwing in the towel?"

"I have to," Quinn said ruefully. "If I keep going you'll have to roll me out of here, and then I won't be any use to you at all." He gestured for the check, and Paul brought it over after a quick stop at the register.

"Giving up so easily?" Paul asked, eyeing his plate.

"I know my limits," Quinn replied.

"You did better than most," Paul said. "I'm impressed."

Quinn patted his formerly flat stomach again, which now sported a slight bulge and felt tight as a drum. "I'll keep that in mind once the heartburn hits," he said drily.

Paul laughed and removed the plate while Rebecca finished eating. "Men," she muttered, shaking her head as she dug in her purse. She pulled out her wallet, but Quinn shook his head and grabbed the check.

"I've got this."

She glanced up, surprise written on her face. "There's no need," she said. "I can expense it."

"I know, but I insist." Even though this was by no means a date, the idea of letting her pay for his meal made Quinn feel a little funny inside. *Probably the jalapeños*, he told himself. But just the same, he insisted on paying for them both.

He blinked as they stepped outside, the sun blinding after their time in the restaurant. "Where to now?" he asked. "Campground or bar?"

"Campground first," Rebecca said decisively. "I want to at least see where she was living, maybe talk to the neighbors. Then we can head to the bar and chat with Dan before he opens."

"Sounds like a plan." They walked back to the car, and he could tell by the bounce in her step she was excited about this lead.

"You sure you're up for it?" She glanced at him after they were both in the car, her lips twitching with a smile. "I'd hate to add to your discomfort."

"I'll be fine," Quinn assured her, setting off down the bumpy road. He felt a tingling sensation in his overly full stomach that had nothing to do with his lunch and everything to do with the woman in the passenger seat. He could get used to her teasing, if he wasn't careful.

His brain recognized the danger even as his heart whispered, *What if?*

Chapter 6

The sun was low in the sky by the time Quinn pulled in to the parking lot of the ranger station. Rebecca was glad to see he was looking better; he'd seemed a little green around the gills while they'd explored the campground in Terlingua, but as time had passed, the tight lines of discomfort around his eyes and mouth had eased, and now he looked back to normal.

The trip overall had been a success. Victim number one now had a name: Jenny Owens. She'd been a recent transplant to Terlingua, though no one knew where she'd come from.

"Not my business," one of the other residents of the campground had said. "I asked once, and she said she didn't want to talk about it. Seemed she was maybe running from something, but I wasn't gonna pry."

Even Dan hadn't known much about Jenny's past. But they had enough information now to start a search, and hopefully soon the police would find her family or friends.

"Do you think Jenny was her real name?" Quinn's quiet voice interrupted Rebecca's thoughts, and she turned to look at him in the golden glow of the afternoon light.

Rebecca blew out a breath through pursed lips. "I don't know," she said. "I've been thinking about that, and it's possible she lied. Based on what her neighbor said, it sounds like she was on the run from something. Maybe she gave a false name to try to protect herself." The medical examiner had entered her DNA sequence into the normal databases, but nothing had popped up. Jenny hadn't been running from a criminal history, but there were other kinds of trouble that a person might want to escape.

"That makes your job more complicated, doesn't it?"

She nodded. "Yeah. But I'm going to let the police take the lead now. Hopefully, they can find out more based on the information we gathered today."

"What about the second victim?"

"That's a little harder." Rebecca had hoped to identify both women, but no one they'd spoken to today had recognized the other victim. "Maybe she's from a different town?"

"Anything is possible. Do you want to try another place tomorrow?"

She frowned, considering her options. She was torn between two competing desires—to identify the second victim, and to scout more of the trails Quinn usually patrolled, in a bid to anticipate where the killer might leave another body. "Let's see if the police can take over the search for now," she said, thinking out loud. "There are more of them than us, and they can split up and cover more ground than we can." Some officers could also go back to Terlingua and try to learn more about whom Jenny had been with in her last days—she'd probably met the killer in town, which meant someone must have seen them together.

"What's on our agenda for tomorrow then?"

"I want you to take me on some of the other trails you spend time on," she said. "Walk me through a basic tour of your day. I want to know where you go and what you see. The killer knows your schedule, which means I need to as well."

Quinn swallowed hard. "You think he's going to strike again." It wasn't a question.

Rebecca nodded. "I do. Guys like this don't just stop. He's going to keep going until we catch him."

Quinn was silent for a moment, and she could tell he was shaken by the situation. Her heart went out to him—it wasn't easy to be the one to find one murder victim, let alone two. And the knowledge that he was somehow tied up in this whole situation had to be disturbing at best.

Brandon would have known what to say. He'd always been good at putting people at ease. It was one of the qualities that made him such a fantastic interrogator. But he wasn't here and never would be again. She was on her own.

"What time do you want to start in the morning?"

"The sooner the better. Before it gets too hot."

Quinn nodded his assent. It was on the tip of her tongue to ask him to join her for dinner—he looked like he could use the company and, frankly, she wouldn't mind having someone to talk to, either. There was something about Quinn that made her relax, that eased the knot of tension she seemed to permanently carry in her chest. It was the strangest thing, the way his presence made her feel...safe.

Brandon had done that for her. When she'd been with him, she'd felt like nothing could go wrong. His murder had shattered those illusions, and ever since then, she'd felt raw and exposed. She hadn't expected to ever feel secure again, which was why being around Quinn was such a revelation. Was this simply the next stage in her healing process, or was there something special about Quinn that gave her peace?

It wasn't fair to compare the two men, and truth be told, they were quite different. She was still getting to know Quinn, but she already recognized he lacked Brandon's easy smile and ready charm. Quinn had a quiet charisma that was more subtle. He could put people at their ease, but she suspected he could also use his large size to intimidate. Brandon hadn't been as tall or strong as Quinn—he'd spent his time behind a desk rather than hiking and patrolling the land. Quinn's physical efforts showed in his toned arms and flat stomach, and Rebecca would be lying to herself if she pretended she hadn't noticed.

"Would you—" He paused, then shook his head. "Ah, never mind."

He seemed suddenly shy, and she recalled his words about Rebecca from their initial interview, which now seemed so long ago... *I was so nervous around her that if it had been up to me, I'd probably still be searching for the courage to ask her on that first date.*

Did he want to have dinner with her, too? Or was she simply misreading the situation? Only one way to find out...

"I'm hungry," she announced. "Would you join me for dinner? That is, if you have room in your stomach after today's lunch."

Relief flashed in his eyes, followed quickly by a grin. "I think I can eat something. If you're not too sick of my company yet."

She shook her head. "Hardly. Why don't I follow you back to town?" She would have preferred to ride with him, but this way he didn't need to make a trip back out to the park to drop off her car.

"That works. I know just the place."

He waited while she climbed into her rental and got things started. Then he turned onto the main road that led back to Alpine.

It's not a date, Rebecca told herself as she followed. *Just dinner between two colleagues.* Because that's all they were to each other.

And all they ever could be.

This is...nice.

In truth, it was more than just nice. Having dinner with Rebecca was proving to be one of the most enjoyable things he'd done in recent memory.

Quinn had taken her to one of his favorite places—a little hole-in-the-wall Tex-Mex restaurant. It wasn't much to look at from the outside, but their salsa was to die for, and the tamales were out of this world. Even though he was still feeling a bit full from the monstrosity of a burger he'd tackled earlier, he couldn't resist ordering some *queso* dip for them to share.

"This is fantastic," Rebecca said around a mouthful of food.

He smiled, happy to know she was enjoying her dinner. "You can't come to this part of the country and not enjoy Tex-Mex," he said. "Even people who don't like Tex-Mex have to admit it's pretty good out here."

They spent most of the meal chatting, the conversation light and casual. It was eye-opening to see a different side of Rebecca. Most of the time they had spent together, she'd been focused on the case. Now, her intensity was gone, replaced by a lightness that he found refreshing.

And very attractive.

If he'd thought she was pretty before, seeing her laugh made him realize just how beautiful she truly was. The light over their table made her eyes shine and her skin glow and turned her hair the color of a desert sunset. He could have stared at her all night, soaking up this side of her.

He found himself leaning forward, unconsciously trying to get closer as she told a story about one of her friends back in Virginia. Her body language mirrored his own, and he suddenly realized that to an outside observer, they probably looked like a couple on a date.

The thought sent a little jolt down his spine. He'd been on a few dates since Ashley's death, but none had ever gone this well. He felt a connection to Rebecca that had been lacking with other women. Maybe he'd tried to move on too quickly, or perhaps Rebecca was simply special. Either way, this dinner was going to make it hard to keep his developing feelings under control.

But it doesn't matter how I feel, he realized. Rebecca was a professional, there to do a job. His fascination was one-sided, and he wasn't going to make things awkward for her by admitting to or acting on his attraction. Besides, if he let himself really fall for her, he was only setting himself up for pain later, when she left to go back to Virginia. He'd experienced quite enough heartache in his life already—he wasn't going to sign up for more if he could help it.

The waiter brought their check and he grabbed it

without thinking. Rebecca eyed him over the rim of her glass. "Still not gonna let me pay?"

Quinn shook his head. "Maybe next time."

"I'm going to hold you to that," she replied. "Both the promise of a next time, and the fact you agreed to let me pick up the tab."

A jolt of pleasure went through him at her words. In another time and place, he might have thought she was flirting with him.

It's not a date, he told himself sternly. Sure, they were enjoying a meal together, and yes, he was paying for it. But that had more to do with the manners his mother had drilled into him from a young age than any potential for romance.

Right?

After he paid, they walked outside. The evening air was cool and smelled of desert sage, tinged with a hint of smoke from a campfire somewhere. Nerves fluttered in his stomach at the prospect of saying good-night. If this had been a real date, he'd know what to do—hug her and kiss her cheek. If they had simply been coworkers, he'd say goodbye with a smile and wave. But Rebecca's status wasn't easily classified, and he was uncertain about how he should act.

In the end, it didn't matter. Once they reached their cars, Rebecca turned to face him. She took a deep breath and stepped forward, her arms going around him as she pressed herself against his chest.

"Thanks for your help today," she said softly. She pulled back, studying his face for a moment. Her blue eyes sparkled like stars in the glow of the parking-lot lights. Before he could respond, she rose to her toes and pressed a soft kiss to the corner of his mouth.

Quinn froze, his breath caught in his throat. Rebecca slipped out of his arms with a shy smile. "See you in the morning."

"Yes," he said, his voice sounding like the croak of a dying frog. He swallowed, trying to act normal. Rebecca probably hadn't meant anything by the kiss, but the simple contact had thrown him for a loop. He waited while she got into her car, watched her start it up and head off. He said goodbye with a wave, his feet planted in the gravel of the parking lot and his heart still pounding in his chest.

"She was just being friendly," he told himself. "Nothing more."

But no matter how many times he said it, his heart refused to give up hope.

Three hours later...

"How much longer? I can't really see anything out here." Crystal's voice was teetering on the edge of a whine, and he clenched his jaw. *Soon*, he told himself. Soon enough he would be rid of this troublesome woman.

"Not too far," he told her, striving to keep his tone friendly. "Trust me, the view will be worth the hike. When you see the comet, you'll be amazed."

"If you say so," she muttered. They walked on

in silence for a few more moments before she spoke again. "What did you say the comet was called again?"

"It's the Voyager comet," he lied.

She hummed thoughtfully. "I don't remember hearing anything about it on the news."

"It comes around once every couple of years," he said, thinking fast. "Not really a big deal."

"I guess," she said skeptically.

Her suspicion was well-founded, but it was too little, too late. Now that he had her on the trail, it was just the two of them. They were alone, with no one around for miles.

Just the way he liked it.

She stumbled a bit on some loose rocks. He reached out to steady her, and she shot him a grateful smile. "Thanks," she said. "I'm not used to walking around in the dark."

"You won't have to worry about it for much longer," he promised.

His heart began to pound as they approached the site, but not from exertion. It was anticipation that sent his blood racing and warmed him from the inside out. He felt a flush creep over his skin and was grateful for the dim moonlight that kept him in shadows. His fingertips tingled as he pictured wrapping his hands around her throat, imagining the supple give of the tissues in her neck as he squeezed. Quinn's face flashed before his eyes and he grinned, wishing he could witness the moment the park ranger discovered this new offering.

"It's just up ahead," he said, sounding a little breathless even to his own ears.

They rounded a bend and he indicated a large boulder off to the side of the trail. He sat on the still-warm surface of the rock and patted the spot beside him. Crystal lowered herself next to him, her head tilted up as she examined the sky.

"I don't see anything." She sounded unhappy, and any reservations he had about killing her vanished. They'd spent a few enjoyable hours together, enough that he'd started to feel a slight twinge of guilt at the idea of hurting her. But it was something that had to be done, and after listening to her complain tonight, he no longer had any qualms about what he was going to do.

"It'll be here soon," he said. "Keep watching." He stood and she jerked her head around.

"Where are you going?" There was a note of alarm in her voice. "You can't just leave me out here by myself! It can't be safe."

"I'm going to step away for a minute and relieve myself. You'll be fine."

She relaxed a bit, but still looked uncomfortable. "Don't take too long," she said. "It's kind of creepy out here in the dark."

"You have nothing to worry about," he said. "No critter is going to sneak up on you. I promise." A little thrill went through him at the words. If she only knew the truth of her situation…

He walked a few feet away and tended to his business. He wasn't worried about leaving any evidence—what the ground didn't soak up, the morning sun would evaporate before long. By the time Crystal was found, there would be no indication he'd been here at all.

Well, except for her body. He nearly giggled at the thought. A surge of giddiness rose in his system like bubbles in a champagne glass. The idea of champagne was appealing—perhaps he deserved a treat after this? It wouldn't be hard to find a liquor store, and if he paid cash there would be no record of his purchase. Yes, he decided, zipping his pants. A celebration was in order. He'd been working hard the past few weeks; he'd earned a moment's enjoyment.

But first, business.

He turned back to see Crystal was still sitting on the rock, her face tilted toward the sky as she searched in vain for a comet that would never appear. A warm rush of tenderness flooded his chest as he watched her, just as it had when he'd taken one last look at his earlier victims. He wasn't a monster. He simply had a job to do, and these women had their own parts to play in this tale. If anyone was in the wrong, it was Quinn Gallagher.

Anger flared as the park ranger's face appeared in his mind once again. If not for Gallagher, none of this would have happened. He was the reason those women were dead, the reason more would continue to die. Quinn had ruined his life, and he wasn't going to stop until he'd returned the favor.

But none of that mattered now. He couldn't let his

hatred and anger toward Gallagher ruin this final, special moment. If nothing else, he owed it to Crystal to be fully present with her, to keep her company on this final walk.

He slipped on the gloves and stepped carefully, quietly, as he returned to the boulder. No sense spooking her. She'd realize what was happening soon enough.

He stopped just behind her, studying the glow of the moonlight on her hair. It looked almost black in the silver light, not the right color at all. But no matter.

A bug chirruped nearby, making her jump. "John?" she called out uncertainly. "Are you almost done?"

"Yes," he whispered. She let out a shriek, but before she could do so much as turn her head, he snaked his arm around her and put her in a choke hold. She clawed at his forearm, her nails digging for purchase as she tried to fight him off. The excess fabric of his long-sleeved shirt protected his skin and made her struggles useless. In a matter of seconds, she went limp, her body leaning back into his chest as she lost consciousness.

He lowered her down until she was lying on the rock, her hair streaming down the sides like an ebony waterfall. He allowed himself a few seconds to study her—she looked so peaceful there in the dark. Then he reached for her neck, gripping tightly as he squeezed the last gasps of life from her body.

Chapter 7

"How'd you sleep?" Quinn greeted Rebecca the next morning with a smile, handing her a cup of coffee. Rebecca forced herself to take it smoothly from his hand, resisting the temptation to snatch it out of his grip and down the contents in one go like some kind of feral animal.

"Fine," she lied, hoping the concealer she'd applied this morning was doing a sufficient job of hiding the dark circles under her eyes. In truth, she hadn't slept much at all. Between thoughts of the case and reliving their dinner, her brain simply hadn't been willing to shut down and allow her to rest.

I shouldn't have kissed him, she told herself for probably the millionth time. She'd let herself get caught up in the pleasure of the moment—they'd shared such a nice meal, with good conversation and lots of laughter, despite the shadow of the case hanging over their heads. It had been so long since she'd experienced anything like that. Even though it hadn't been a date, it had definitely *felt* like one. And when he'd reached for the check again, she couldn't help but feel a little flattered.

So as they'd stood in the parking lot, the full moon just starting to ascend in the sky, Rebecca had thrown caution to the wind. She'd meant for the hug and kiss to be nothing more than a friendly good-night, a means of thanking him for his efforts during the day and for treating her to another meal. Hopefully, Quinn had interpreted it that way.

Too bad her body had gotten the wrong idea.

Feeling his broad chest pressed against her had lit sparks in her limbs that even now glowed like bright embers, ready and waiting for the opportunity to burst into flames. The misaligned kiss she'd given him had been a strange mix of sensations—the softness of his lips combined with a slight rasp of stubble on his skin. His scent had filled her nose—warm skin, a hint of detergent and a whiff of desert sage. Even though the embrace hadn't lasted more than a few seconds, it had been enough to make her head spin and her body sit up and take notice.

So much for her resolve to keep her distance.

But I haven't crossed the line. The realization had come to her in the early hours of the morning. Sure, she was dancing on the edge of the boundary between professional and personal, but she hadn't stepped over it. Not yet, anyway. She could still pull back, retreat into the safety of rules and regulations and code-of-conduct statements.

But she couldn't silence the small voice in her heart that wondered...*what if*?

Quinn was the first man she'd felt drawn to since Brandon's death. Was she doing herself a disservice by trying to pretend she didn't feel anything? Was it right for her to ignore her emotions when she might never feel this way again?

The questions had plagued her all night, and the answers were elusive and out of reach. The one thing she knew for sure was that she would have to make a decision soon, if only for her own peace of mind. This emotional limbo was exhausting and counter-productive. One way or another, she needed to choose how to proceed with Quinn—to keep things strictly professional, or cautiously explore what might lie between them.

It didn't help that he looked handsome as ever this morning, or that he'd been waiting with coffee. His brown eyes practically shone with warmth as he watched her drink, as if he was enjoying the sight of her sipping something he'd made.

"This is great," she said. "Thank you."

"No problem," he replied. "I needed a few cups to get going myself, so I figured I'd have one waiting for you. Share the wealth, and all that."

A few cups, hmmm? she mused. Did that mean he'd had his own troubles sleeping last night?

"Which trail would you like to explore today?" He led her to his desk, and gestured to a map of the park. Highlighted yellow lines snaked over the terrain. "These are the ones I'm usually responsible for," he said, pointing at the marked routes. "This one is where I found the first victim, and this is the one we hiked the other day."

That left several more paths to consider. Rebecca frowned as she studied the map. The trails the killer had already used weren't especially close to each other, so he probably wasn't picking them based on proximity. They had both been fairly strenuous, though, which had likely suited him just fine. The tougher the course, the less chance of coming across other hikers while he was with the victim, either before or after her death. Given his choice of trails, he was probably an experienced hiker, a likelihood she added to her mental profile of the murderer.

She said as much to Quinn. He nodded. "Then I think we should try this one." His finger landed on a route, tapping it for emphasis. "This trail is rated moderate, while the others are considered easy or beginner level. If you think he's picking them based on difficulty, this is probably the one he'd go for next."

"Then that's the trail we'll check out first," she declared.

It didn't take long to collect their packs and load up on water. The sun was still climbing in the sky as they set out, and the light breeze held a hint of chill that triggered goose bumps on Rebecca's arms. She shivered a bit, grateful for the light jacket she wore. Quinn chuckled.

"Enjoy it while it lasts," he said. "You know how warm it can get here."

"That's true," she replied. "I'm not complaining."

They walked without speaking for a few minutes, birdsong and the chirping of unseen insects providing a soundtrack as they moved. Finally, Quinn asked, "What exactly are you hoping to find on the trail?"

"Nothing," she replied. "But what I'd like to do is stake out positions where we can install motion-triggered cameras, or perhaps even camouflage a police officer who can monitor activity along the path. The first two women were killed exactly a week apart, which means we have a little time before he's going to strike again. If we have someone waiting for him, we should be able to stop him before he makes another move"

"That would be great," Quinn said. He sounded almost relieved, and clearly hoped the ordeal would be over soon.

Rebecca sympathized—the sooner she wrapped up this case, the better, at least from the perspective of saving lives. But part of her was reluctant to leave Quinn and the possibilities he represented.

Don't get ahead of yourself. She couldn't take for granted this approach was going to actually catch the killer. He'd been smart so far, and it was probably going to take a healthy dose of luck to trap him in the act. Still, she felt good about this strategy; it definitely had the potential to work.

They reached the top of a small incline and began to descend. Rebecca's gaze snagged on a flash of color about a hundred yards away. She squinted, trying to bring it into focus. At this distance, she couldn't make out the object, but the flash of bright blue was unnatural and out of place in this landscape of browns, reds and oranges.

She stopped, dread filling her stomach and weighing down her limbs. Quinn drew up next to her. "What's wrong?" His face was etched with concern as he looked at her. He reached out, placing his hands on her shoulders. "Are you okay? Do you feel sick?"

Rebecca shook her head, knowing she had to tell him but wishing she could avoid it. He'd taken the first two deaths so hard… Finding a third body was going to really hurt him.

"I—I think I see something." She swallowed and jerked her chin in the direction of the trail. "Down there."

His face drained of color and he tightened his grip on her shoulders. "I see." He turned to look, scanning the terrain ahead. She felt him jerk and knew he'd seen what she had.

"Let me go check it out," she said, reaching up to cover one of his hands with her own. "It might be nothing. Maybe some trash."

"Maybe," he said, but they both knew it was a lie.

"I'll be right back."

"No." He kept his hands on her, refusing to let go even as she took a step down the path. "No, I'm not letting you go alone."

"Quinn, you don't have to see this."

He smiled, but there was no joy in the expression. "I know what it's like to find them," he said, his voice barely above a whisper. "I'm not letting you do that alone. Besides, what if the killer is still around, watching and waiting?"

It was a possibility, but Rebecca doubted it. The man wasn't ready to be caught yet, and he wouldn't take a chance of being discovered. "Are you sure?"

He nodded, his spine straightening. "Yes. We do this together."

"I hope I'm wrong," she said as they set off down the trail.

"I hope so, too."

But she wasn't.

He pressed the binoculars to his eyes, his gaze locked on the scene below.

Quinn was walking toward the body, his stiff movements making it clear he knew what he was going to find. He smiled as he watched Quinn approach. "This time is different," he said to himself. "I hope you enjoy your little gift, Gallagher."

After strangling Crystal and arranging her body in the characteristic position, he'd left a message for Quinn. Nothing more than his name spelled out in small rocks and words scrawled in the dirt, but hope-fully it was enough to get under the man's skin.

He'd climbed up to this vantage point a few hours ago, needing to watch the scene for the moment of discovery. He hadn't been able to spy on the first two victims, and in truth, he hadn't known for certain if Quinn would be the one to discover this one. But it seemed luck was on his side...

Who was the woman with Quinn, though? Lovely red hair, almost the exact shade he tried to find... The pair of them walked together, and as they ap-proached the body, he saw her take Quinn's hand in a gesture of support. She clearly knew what to ex-pect, but she didn't seem flustered or too upset. A professional, then, he surmised. A cop? Maybe even a federal agent?

Pleasure bloomed in his chest at the thought that his actions were receiving national attention. But the sensation was quickly snuffed out. It was only one woman; if the authorities were really taking him se-riously, there should be a task force involved, not a lone officer probably dispatched as a matter of course.

He took a deep breath, pushing aside his disap-pointment and anger. This was simply the beginning. It was going to take time to ruin Gallagher's life, and succumbing to impatience would only wreck his plan.

They had reached the body now. Quinn and the woman were crouched down, clearly talking. Quinn had his radio to his mouth and she pulled out a cell phone. They were likely calling in the authorities, which meant it was time for him to leave. He was far enough away that he wasn't worried about being seen, but he didn't want to risk running into any police as they made their way to the site. Besides, he had other plans…

He smiled as he began to walk down the mountain trail. *Stay tuned, Quinn. This isn't over yet.*

Chapter 8

"You okay?"

Quinn jerked his shoulder in a shrug, keeping his eyes on the trail in front of them. It was midafternoon and the police had just finished collecting the body. The team from the coroner's office pushed a gurney over the rocky terrain, their pace awkward and slow. Quinn and Rebecca trailed a respectful distance behind the procession as they headed back to the ranger station.

"As good as I can be, under the circumstances," he said finally. Part of him still couldn't believe there was another body, another woman dead. The needless loss of life both angered and saddened him in equal measure. He'd never seen this woman before, but she looked young, like the others. She should be working or going to college, dreaming about future plans. Not zipped into a body bag being jostled down a trail.

"This is the first time he's left you a message." It wasn't a question, but Quinn nodded.

"Yes." As if finding the young woman hadn't been bad enough. Quinn had felt a literal shock zap his system when he'd seen his name spelled out in small rocks. The killer had also used a stick or something similar to etch out a message in the dirt—*having fun yet?*

The question was grotesque and out of place, considering the situation. Quinn swallowed hard as he pictured the words, feeling like he'd been punched in the gut. There was no denying it now—the killer was definitely targeting him, as sure as he was picking off those innocent women. But who would do such a thing? And why was this psycho involving Quinn in his sick deeds?

"I think it's time we take a hard look at your associates and friends," Rebecca said.

"My friends would never do something like this," he said reflexively. It made him sick to his stomach to think that someone he cared about and spent time with was capable of committing such heinous acts. Surely the type of person who killed without remorse would bear some kind of mark or display a sign of their internal evil, something to warn people away.

Rebecca's earlier words flashed through his mind: *Like it or not, we have more in common with these guys than we care to admit.* Logically, he knew she was right. But he couldn't accept the idea that one of his friends could be responsible for these crimes.

"I know it's difficult to imagine the killer is someone you know," Rebecca said softly. "But whoever is doing this has singled you out. And his behavior is escalating."

Quinn frowned. "Escalating? You mean, because of the message?"

Rebecca nodded. "That, and the fact he's killed again so soon. The interval between the first two victims was one week. This woman was targeted after only five days. The next victim might appear in five days, if he's setting a new pattern, or he might strike again before that."

Quinn's heart dropped. "Oh, God," he whispered.

"He wants your attention," Rebecca said. "He's not content for you to be a passive participant anymore. He left that message deliberately to draw you in, to force you to respond."

"If I give him what he wants, will he stop killing?" Maybe there was something he could do, something he could say that would appease this sicko and keep his future victims safe. The thought of engaging with such a monster filled him with disgust, but he would do it if that's what was necessary.

"No." Rebecca didn't hesitate, and her answer left no room for doubt. "He's not going to stop, no matter what he might say. But if you do engage with him, it might distract him enough to get him to make a mistake."

"How do I do that? We don't even know who he is. It's not like I can call him up and say, 'What do you want from me?'"

"True, but we can craft a response and have you interviewed by the local news stations. Maybe even put out a message that the killer might see."

Quinn nodded, feeling defeated. "Do what you think is best. I'll cooperate."

Her touch was light on his arm, but he drew comfort from the contact nonetheless. "I know you will."

"I'll draw up a list of my friends and coworkers," he said. "They won't be hard to find."

"What about enemies?" Rebecca asked. "Whoever is doing this is trying to hurt you. Can you think of anyone who might be motivated to cause you harm?"

Quinn considered the question, thinking about all the people he knew. "I don't usually make it a point to socialize with people who don't seem to like me," he said. And he generally shied away from the kind of drama that would lead to making enemies.

"What about coworkers?" Rebecca persisted. "Were you promoted over anyone, or has anything happened that might leave someone with hard feelings?"

"Well…" He trailed off as a few possibilities occurred to him. "I did get a title bump last summer. Nothing major, but there were three of us being considered and I was the one they picked."

"Anything else?"

He frowned, remembering. "I have had a few run-ins with some hikers," he admitted. "There's a group of young men who play fast and loose with safety and the rules of the park—I've caught them several times violating the burn ban, and have had to be the bad guy when it comes to enforcing park rules."

"How did they respond?"

"Not well," he admitted. "Last time I ran into them was a little over a month ago. It almost came to blows."

"Did they threaten you?" Rebecca sounded interested, as if he was on the right track.

"Just the usual taunts young guys throw out when they're drunk and acting tough for their friends." He recounted what they'd said, trying to leave out the worst of the profanity.

"I'll need names," she declared. "And we need to find them. Maybe we can check out their campsite."

Quinn's knee-jerk response was to refuse. He didn't have a problem telling Rebecca the names of the guys who'd given him trouble, but he didn't want her going anywhere near them. They were unpredictable at best, dangerous at worst. And if they really were behind these killings? She'd be in incredible danger. Better to let the police arrest them and have her question them under controlled circumstances.

"Why don't you let the local police pick them up?" he suggested carefully. He didn't want to offend Rebecca or imply she wasn't capable of doing her job, but he also wanted to keep her far away from potential trouble. The young men already had a grudge against him, and if he showed up unannounced to their campsite with Rebecca in tow, there was no telling how they'd respond. There were three of them to his one, and if it came down to a fight, he wouldn't be able to protect her.

She lifted one eyebrow as she regarded him. "Worried I can't handle myself?"

He shook his head. "Not at all. I just don't think we need to go borrowing trouble. I'd rather not provoke them, and I think you'll have better luck getting information from them if I'm not there."

"You're probably right," she said, tilting her head in acknowledgment. "It'll be easier to talk to him if they're not posturing for your benefit."

He thought back to his last encounter with the group, the way the young men had puffed out their chests and fed off each other's aggression. The idea that their display had been for his benefit nearly made him laugh. He'd been twenty once, full of confidence. He'd thought he could take on the world as well, but he'd never flirted with violence the way these kids did. *Testosterone poisoning*, said his mother's voice in his head.

All the more reason to keep them away from Rebecca.

"What else can we do?" He needed to act, to do something to help the investigation. If he had to sit at a desk and think about those poor women, he'd go mad. Better to keep moving, to feel like he was contributing, even if only in a small way.

Rebecca sighed, her gaze landing on the gurney ahead of them. They'd almost reached the trailhead, and the coroner's team was having an easier time maneuvering the wheels along the ground. "I'm going to call for some reinforcements," she said. "It's clear the local police are out of their depth here—the department is just too small to handle all the different directions of this investigation. We need assistance if we're going to catch this guy."

"I guess that means you won't need my help anymore." He tried to keep the disappointment out of his voice. It had been clear from the start she was only going to be in his life temporarily. Better for them to part ways now, before his feelings grew even further.

"On the contrary," she said. "Something tells me you're the key to this entire investigation. I'm not letting you out of my sight." Her tone held a teasing note, but Quinn could tell she was serious.

They walked in silence the rest of the way, each lost in their own thoughts. They followed the gurney into the parking lot and watched as the team loaded the body into the back of a van. Rebecca shuddered a bit, and Quinn put his hand on her shoulder.

"You okay?" She'd been so composed and focused all day, it hadn't occurred to him she might be upset as well. He knew from experience how difficult it was to find a body, but he'd figured Rebecca was too professional to let her emotions cloud her thoughts and actions.

"I'm fine," she said. "I'm not used to being the first one on the scene. I generally don't interact with the victims in person—I usually just see crime-scene photos, which are much more removed from the situation."

He pulled gently on her shoulder and she stepped into his arms with a small sigh. "I'm sorry you had to see that," he said softly.

She wrapped her arms around him and burrowed close. "Same to you," she said. "I can only imagine how tough it's been for you to go through that several times in the past two weeks."

"It's hard," he said. And while today's discovery had been horrible, he didn't feel that same clawing desperation that had plagued him after the discovery of the first two victims. Maybe he was growing desensitized. Or maybe it had something to do with the woman in his arms.

Rebecca's presence had helped him today. Even though they hadn't spent much time in conversation, just having her nearby had calmed him. He'd drawn strength from her measured reactions, the business-like way she'd set about doing her job. He'd taken his cues from her, and she'd kept him grounded today so that his emotions hadn't spun off out of control.

Now it seemed it was his turn to help her.

She wasn't the type to complain—he knew that much. But it was clear she was feeling the effects of their discovery and he wanted to ease her mind, make her feel normal again, if only for a few minutes.

"I know you're probably not hungry, but we need to eat." They'd stayed at the site most of the day, missing lunch. The lack of food and the heat had left him feeling drained, and he imagined she was feeling the same way.

She nodded, her head moving against his chest. "Actually, I could really use a drink."

Quinn didn't blame her. He wasn't much of a drinker himself, but a little alcohol might help both of them take the edge off of the day. "I know just the place."

At first glance, the Flowering Cactus wasn't much to look at. The place was at the end of a strip of doughnut shops and dry cleaners in Alpine, tacked on almost like an afterthought. The sign simply said BAR, and a neon cactus flickered in one of the windows, casting a green glow on the sidewalk.

Rebecca looked at Quinn, who smiled slightly and shrugged. "Just wait," he advised.

He held the door and they walked inside. The bar was surprisingly well lit, with a stage at the far end. A small group of men were mulling about, holding guitars, setting up microphones and corralling a network of cords that stretched across the floor. Rebecca mentally braced herself for the aural onslaught that was sure to come—after all, how good could this small local band really be?

She and Quinn snagged a small table against the wall and she reached for the laminated menu stuck between the condiment bottles.

"There's not much to choose from," he said as she glanced down the page. "But the food isn't bad."

A moment later a young woman approached the table for their order. "You should try the local brew," Quinn advised. "That's what this place is known for."

"Sounds good," Rebecca said. The waitress scribbled down their requests and left. Quinn leaned forward, elbows on the table.

"Doing okay?"

Rebecca nodded. In truth, she wasn't sure how she felt at the moment. Finding the third victim had been upsetting, and she was a little surprised at how much it bothered her. Rebecca was no stranger to death—in her line of work, she routinely looked at crime-scene photos and autopsy reports, and she often listened to the killers themselves recount the details of their crimes. But there was something different about stumbling across a victim so soon after the murder. She was used to having a wall of separation between herself and the crime—photos were graphic, yes, but they were still removed from the actual event. It was tougher to compartmentalize her emotions when she was sitting next to the body, the scent of death fresh in her nose.

The waitress deposited their drinks and fluttered away again. Rebecca took a sip. "You're right," she said, taking a deeper draw. "This *is* good."

Quinn smiled. "Glad you like it."

The alcohol hit her right away, likely thanks to a combination of hunger and being out in the heat all day. Her limbs tingled pleasantly as warmth spread through her system. She forced herself to put down the glass—it was tempting to drink it all in one go, but she wanted to enjoy this feeling of relaxation and not slip right into drunkenness.

"How are you?" she asked. This was Quinn's third time finding a body, and she could tell by the haunted look in his brown eyes it weighed on him.

He lifted a shoulder in a shrug, trying to look casual. "I've had better days." He sipped his own beer, studying her over the rim of the glass. "I'm a little worried," he confessed. "I really don't want this to become the new normal."

"It won't," she said, trying to inject confidence into her voice. Rebecca took pride in her ability to do her job well, but now wasn't the time to discuss the fact that she didn't always catch the bad guy.

"Quinn! Good to see you, buddy!"

They both glanced up. A tall, handsome man stood at their table, a wide grin on his face. Quinn stood and shook his hand, clapping him on the back.

"How's it going, Carter?"

"Doing well. Glad you made it out." He turned to the table and stuck out his hand. "Carter Donaghey."

Rebecca introduced herself. "Carter is another ranger," Quinn explained. "He mainly works in the far west region of the park."

"That explains why I haven't met you before now," Rebecca said.

"Better late than never," Carter said, winking at her.

Rebecca felt her face flush and hoped it wasn't too obvious. Carter was definitely cute, and under any other circumstances, she would have appreciated his flirting. But his easygoing charm was no match for the thoughtful care Quinn had shown over the past few days.

"I need to get back over there," Carter said, jerking his head in the direction of the stage. "We're gonna start soon. I just wanted to say hi."

"Nice to meet you," Rebecca said. Carter and Quinn said their goodbyes, and Carter walked away.

"Sorry," Quinn said after the other man had left. "I didn't know he'd be playing here tonight."

"It's no problem," she said. "He seems like a nice guy."

"He is," Quinn confirmed. "I don't know him that well, but every time I see him he's always friendly."

"I wonder if he's seen anything that might help with the investigation," she mused. "It's possible the killer is hanging out in another area of the park between murders to avoid detection."

"Maybe," Quinn said. "But let's worry about that later. You can't exactly interview him now, and I brought you here to help take your mind off things, remember?"

She ducked her head, feeling a little sheepish.

"You're right. I have a hard time switching out of work mode sometimes." It was something Brandon had nagged her about frequently, to the point of annoyance. She appreciated the fact Quinn's reminder had been a gentle nudge rather than a blatant demand for her attention.

They fell into an easy conversation, interrupted a few minutes later by the arrival of their food. Carter and his friends took the stage while they ate. "Howdy, y'all. Thanks for coming out tonight. We're Tall Cotton, and we're gonna get started."

Rebecca braced herself, but the band was surprisingly good. They played a mix of original songs and popular covers that had her toe tapping to the beat. Carter had a nice voice, and she saw more than one woman in the audience eyeing him appreciatively. The area in front of the stage was clear of tables and chairs and the small dance floor was soon crowded with couples swaying to the music.

Quinn gave her a questioning look. Rebecca nodded, her stomach fluttering with nerves as she stood to take his hand. What was she doing? She didn't know the first thing about dancing. And to her untrained eye, it looked like some of the people were starting an impromptu line dance, which was even more complicated.

He led her to a corner of the floor and brought her close. "Uh, I have a confession to make."

"What's that?" His brown eyes flickered with

amusement, and she had a feeling he already knew what she was about to say.

"I don't know how to dance."

"That's all right." He placed one hand on her hip, a large, warm weight that anchored her to him. "I'll teach you. Just relax."

She placed one hand on his shoulder and fitted her other hand into his. Then he began to guide them to the music, gently nudging her in one direction or another.

Rebecca moved stiffly at first, trying to anticipate and control where they moved. Quinn brought her even closer and dipped his head. "Relax," he whispered in her ear. "I've got you."

Maybe it was the heat of his body seeping into hers. Maybe it was the scent of him filling her nose. Or perhaps it was simply the alcohol taking effect, draining the tension from her muscles. For whatever reason, Rebecca surrendered to Quinn's lead, her body melting against his as he guided them across the floor.

The band transitioned to another song. Quinn's rhythm changed. "Let's try a little two-step," he said softly. Rebecca didn't resist this time, following his lead as he introduced the new steps. Soon, they were gliding along in sync, as if they'd been dancing together for years.

She lost track of time as they moved, the music fading into the background as she focused on the feel of Quinn's arms around her. There was something so good, so right, about the way he held her, the way their bodies fit together. Almost as if they were made for each other.

It was a fanciful thought, one she wanted to dismiss immediately. But she couldn't deny the pull Quinn exerted on her, or the way his presence eased the small part of her heart that always felt like a tightly coiled spring on the verge of snapping.

I could get used to this, she realized. Spending time with Quinn made her see how one-dimensional her life in Virginia had been. Sure, she had friends and went out occasionally, but the bulk of her time was spent on work. While that hadn't bothered her before, she now recognized she'd been hiding from the world. It had been so easy to dedicate herself to the job, to the detriment of her personal life. Relationships required care and attention, things she hadn't felt capable of providing in the wake of Brandon's death.

But being around Quinn made her think she was ready to try again.

Did he feel the same way? Was he open to the possibility of something new? Or was he still focused on grieving, devoted to the memory of his wife?

The music drew to a close. Quinn stepped back, putting some space between them. He smiled down at her, emotions she couldn't name flickering through his eyes. "Thirsty?"

"Yes."

She dimly heard Carter saying something about

taking a break as they walked back to their table. The beer was now warm, but it was wet and went down easily. She opened her mouth to speak, but was beaten to the punch by a new arrival.

"I thought that was you."

They both turned at the voice. A slight man stood next to the table, his light brown hair a bit on the longish side. "It is you, right? Quinn Gallagher?"

Rebecca glanced at Quinn, who was staring up at the new arrival with his mouth slightly open. "Justin?"

The man smiled. "The one and only."

"My God," Quinn said softly. Then he jumped to his feet and stuck out his hand, clapping the other man on the back. "It's good to see you! What are you doing here?" Quinn snagged a nearby chair, pulling it over to the table. Justin sat and shrugged.

"I got some time off work and decided to come down here for a little camping and hiking. A friend was here last summer and said the views were amazing."

"They are," Quinn confirmed. He glanced at Rebecca. "I'm sorry, we're being rude. Rebecca, this is Justin. Naomi's husband."

It took a few seconds for her to process the significance of the name, but then she remembered. Naomi had been friends with Ashley, Quinn's wife. She was the woman who had died in the same accident that killed Ashley. "Nice to meet you," she said, smiling.

"Likewise," Justin replied. He turned back to Quinn.

"I think I remember hearing you'd moved to Big Bend, but I never thought I'd actually run in to you."

"It's a small world," Quinn said. "How have you been?"

The two men chatted for a few minutes, catching up. Rebecca watched Quinn closely as they talked. She could tell from his reaction he'd been shocked to see Justin. Quinn appeared happy enough to talk to the other man, but she noted the subtle lines of strain around his eyes and the way his smile looked just a bit forced. Seeing Naomi's widower out of the blue had probably brought up a lot of emotions he hadn't been prepared to confront, and her heart went out to him.

Please go, she thought silently. Justin seemed nice enough, but she didn't like to see Quinn upset. They'd been having such a nice evening but now the glow was gone. Could they recapture a bit of the spark before saying good-night? She hated the thought of sending him home alone to deal with the consequences of this emotional ambush. Maybe they could get a coffee somewhere, or catch a movie…

"Well, I didn't mean to interrupt," Justin said, rising to his feet. "Just wanted to say hi."

Quinn stood as well. "It was good to see you," he said. "Maybe we can get together for dinner while you're in the area."

"I'd like that," Justin replied. He nodded at Rebecca. "I'm glad to see you're moving on."

Quinn blushed but didn't reply. Rebecca bit her

tongue, settling instead for a bland smile. "Take care," she said.

Rebecca studied Quinn as he watched Justin walk away. She could only imagine how he must feel right now, after that unexpected blast from the past. Should she ask him about it, or would he prefer to pretend nothing had happened? Although she felt like she already knew Quinn well, there was still a lot about him that remained a mystery.

After a few seconds of internal debate, Rebecca decided to speak up. If he didn't want to talk, at least he knew she was willing to listen. "So that was a surprise, huh?"

Quinn startled at the sound of her voice. He shook his head, reminding her of a dog casting off water. Then he turned to her with a small smile. "You can say that again." His tone was light, but his brow was still slightly furrowed.

"Want to talk about it?"

He shook his head again. "Nothing to talk about, really. To tell you the truth, after the funeral, I never thought I'd see him again."

"He probably thought the same thing," she said.

"Maybe so." Quinn shrugged, then drained the last of his beer. Carter and his band took the stage again, and Quinn glanced at her. "Ready to head out? Or would you rather stay…?" He trailed off, but Rebecca recognized he was making the offer simply to be polite. It was clear Quinn didn't want to stick around after the impromptu meeting, and she didn't blame him. The special moment they'd shared before was gone, and the magic wouldn't return once the band started playing again.

"We can go." She dug a few bills out of her purse and left them on the table. For once, Quinn didn't protest. Another sign he was feeling off after seeing Justin again. Rebecca's heart ached for him, but what could she do? She knew how grief worked. One minute, she felt fine, like things were finally getting back to normal. Then she heard a song, passed by a café, smelled something familiar...and bam! She was back in that dark hole, trying to claw her way to the light again as if no time had passed at all. It was probably the same for Quinn.

Part of her wanted to turn away, to give him a bit of privacy as he dealt with his emotions. She'd certainly never enjoyed having witnesses to her pain when she'd been going through the worst after Brandon's death. But she didn't want to abandon Quinn while he faced his demons. She cared about him too much to leave him alone right now.

They reached the parking lot, her mind racing as she considered her next move. "You up for a cup of coffee?"

"Nah." He shook his head. "Think I'll just head home and see if there's a baseball game on TV."

Rebecca nodded, trying not to feel hurt by his rejection. "Sounds good."

They stood there for a moment, neither one of them making a move to leave. Finally, Rebecca stepped forward and wrapped her arms around him in a goodbye hug.

Quinn held her close, his heartbeat a steady rhythm in her ear. She felt him relax as the tension drained out of his muscles and he gave himself over to her embrace.

She wasn't sure how long they stood there, wrapped in each other's arms. Time seemed to stand still, the sounds of evening traffic and the symphony of desert bugs fading into insignificance. Her senses were filled with everything Quinn—his touch, his scent, his warmth. She'd initiated the hug to offer him comfort, but she drew strength from him as well.

He pulled back slightly, so she eased her grip to let him go. To her surprise, he didn't step away. They stayed close, Quinn's head low as he looked down at her.

Anticipation sparked between them as the moment grew heavy with possibility. Rebecca sensed Quinn was debating what to do next, and her stomach fluttered with nerves. *Kiss me*, she pleaded silently. She wanted to feel his lips on hers more than anything, but given his current emotional state, he needed to be the one to make the first move.

And after what seemed like an eternity of heartbeats, he did.

The kiss started out soft, a brush of lips that was shy, almost questioning. Quinn seemed to be holding himself back, as if he wasn't sure how Rebecca would respond to this new overture. She tried to match his low intensity, but her desire for more soon took over. She fisted her hands in the fabric of his shirt, locking his mouth against hers. Warmth shot through her, followed by an effervescent tingling that settled low in her belly. Her head spun as she lost herself in the moment, the feel of Quinn's kiss overwhelming her body and mind.

Quinn's need seemed to match her own. His arms tightened around her—they were solid bands that anchored her in place against his chest. He straightened up, bringing her with him until her feet dangled a few inches above the ground. Before she knew what he was doing, he pivoted to deposit her on the hood of her rental car. Her legs parted automatically, and he stepped in as close as the car would allow. She locked her ankles around his knees, further entangling their limbs. She was dimly aware of the fact they were in a public parking lot, but she was too wrapped up in the moment to care.

When Quinn finally pulled back, his breathing was harsh. "Come home with me?" It was part request, part demand. Rebecca could only nod, her lips tingling and her body humming from their kiss. He helped her off the car, then held on to her as her knees wobbled when she tried to stand.

"I've got you," he said softly.

She looked at his face, his brown eyes blazing with desire and heat. But there was more in his gaze—underneath his arousal, she saw tenderness and concern. Her heart flip-flopped in her chest as she realized he truly cared for her. A warmth spread through her limbs that had nothing to do with physical need, and she felt a small jolt in her chest.

Oh, she thought. *So that's what it feels like to fall in love now.*

She'd often wondered if she'd ever find love again after Brandon. She'd assumed that if she did, it would be a Big Deal, an earth-shattering moment she'd be able to see coming from a mile away. But Quinn had slipped under her radar, and somehow she'd moved through like and was rapidly approaching something close to love without knowing it was happening.

A small part of her thought she should be worried. They hadn't known each other for long—could she really be headed for love or was she just experiencing infatuation? *Love,* her heart answered calmly.

Her brain wanted to argue the point, but her heart refused to engage in a discussion. And her body certainly wasn't interested in talking right now, not with Quinn looking at her like she was a delectable dessert he couldn't wait to try. So for once in her life, Rebecca turned off her mind and let her feelings take control.

She slipped her hand into Quinn's with a smile.

"Let's go."

Chapter 9

Quinn unlocked the door to his apartment and stood back so Rebecca could enter first. He caught a whiff of her shampoo as she walked past; the floral scent filled his nose and arousal curled low in his belly.

This is crazy.

The thought had been running through his mind since he'd kissed her in the parking lot. They'd only known each other a few days! But they'd experienced a lot in that short period of time—more than most people shared in years, if ever. And Rebecca didn't feel like a stranger. There was something about her that fit him, as if she was the puzzle piece he hadn't realized he was missing. Being around her brought him a sense of peace he hadn't felt in ages.

In the wake of Ashley's death, Quinn had often wondered if he would ever be capable of loving another woman, of feeling loved in return. Had his wife been the only one for him?

Now he knew the answer.

Rebecca was special—that was undeniable. And while he wasn't sure he could bring himself to say the *L* word just yet, it was only a matter of time before his emotions got the better of his self-preservation.

He followed her into the apartment, locking the door behind them. She had walked into the living room and switched on a lamp, casting a soft glow on the room.

Now that they were alone together, he wasn't sure what to do. He couldn't very well fall on her like a horny teenager, no matter what his body wanted. And it was entirely possible she had changed her mind during the short drive to his apartment. The idea filled him with disappointment, but he would understand if she was having second thoughts.

"Want a drink?" He had a six-pack of beer shoved in the back of his fridge. It was a bit on the older side, but probably still good...

Rebecca shook her head. "You?"

"No, I'm good." He'd had enough at the bar. If they were really going to take things to the next level tonight, he wanted a clear head.

She sat on the sofa and patted the spot next to her. Quinn joined her, feeling suddenly nervous.

Rebecca's blue eyes were clear and bright as she looked at him. "Are we crazy?"

The question was so direct and unexpected, Quinn couldn't help but laugh. "Maybe a little." He shook his head, turning serious. "But this feels right to me."

Rebecca didn't respond, so he continued. "If you're not ready or interested, that's fine. The last thing I want to do is try to pressure you or cajole you. If we're going to do this, it has to be because we both want it."

"I do." Her voice was soft as she glanced away. "But..."

He waited, giving her time and space to think.

After a few seconds she turned back to face him, her expression so vulnerable it made his heart crack. "I haven't been with a man since Brandon died. I don't know how I'm going to react."

Quinn nodded, understanding perfectly. "If it makes you feel any better, it's the same for me. Ashley was the last woman I slept with."

Rebecca's smile was a little wobbly. "So we're both rusty."

"Looks that way." Acting on impulse, Quinn reached out and took one of her hands, holding it between his own. "Like I said, we don't have to do this. But if we do, there's only room for two people in my bed."

"That's only fair," she said.

They were both quiet for a moment, each one lost in thought. Quinn kept waiting to feel a surge of reluctance, expecting that, at any minute, he was going to change his mind. But the sensation never came. The longer he sat next to Rebecca, the more convinced he became that he was doing the right thing.

Ashley was gone. He would always miss her, and a piece of his heart would forever belong to her. But it was time for him to start living again, to stick his neck out and see if he could find happiness with someone else.

"I can't replace her," Rebecca said softly.

Quinn smiled, reaching up to push a strand of hair behind her ear. "I don't want you to," he assured her. "You have your own role to fill." He wasn't looking for a carbon copy of Ashley. He liked Rebecca because of who she was, not because she fit into the wife-shaped hole in his life.

"I know I'm not the same as Brandon," he said.

"No," Rebecca confirmed. "But I don't want you to be."

Her assurance lightened his heart. It seemed like they were both on the same page—neither one of them was looking to relive the experiences of their past. Memories were bound to emerge, but Quinn had no intention of getting lost in his own personal history. He owed it to himself—and Rebecca—to be fully present in the now.

"Thank you." Rebecca brushed his hand with a gentle caress.

"For what?" He was truly puzzled by her gratitude; he hadn't done anything.

"For understanding." She looked relieved and in that moment, he realized how worried she'd been.

Quinn inched closer and wrapped his arms around her. He needed to hold her for a moment, to make it clear that while he wanted her body, he wanted her trust more. Sex could wait. He wasn't interested in a casual fling; it was more important that they both start out with the same understanding and expectations.

She was content to press her head against his chest, snuggling in with a small sigh. His heart warmed with tenderness as he stroked her hair, enjoying the feel of the soft, silky strands against his skin. The simple act of holding her soothed his soul in ways nothing else could and he closed his eyes, savoring the contact between them.

After a few minutes, Rebecca sat up. "Bathroom," she whispered. "Don't go anywhere."

"Not a chance," Quinn responded. He watched her walk away, enjoying the sway of her hips as she moved. His heartbeat picked up speed as anticipation flooded his system. He hadn't felt this potent combination of nerves and excitement since his first time with Ashley. It was yet another sign of how special Rebecca was to him, in case there had been any doubt in his mind.

He moved to the bedroom and kneeled before his bedside table, rummaging in the drawer for protection. He found a few condoms in the back, buried under a couple of books and magazines he'd never gotten around to reading. He studied the crinkled foil wrappers with a critical eye—they didn't *look* damaged, but it was clear they hadn't been treated well. Then he found the date stamped on the package, and his heart sank.

Expired.

Damn.

Maybe they were still good. Some protection had to be better than none, right? But he dismissed the thought immediately. He wasn't going to take chances with Rebecca, not yet anyway. Neither one of them needed a baby right now.

He heard the bathroom door open and her footsteps sounded in the hall. "Quinn?"

"I'm back here," he called out. Might as well tell her the news right away.

She poked her head into the bedroom, her questioning expression clearing when she saw the condoms in his hand. "Oh, good," she said, smiling. "I don't have any."

"Don't celebrate just yet," he warned. "They're expired."

"Oh." Her face fell, mirroring his own disappointment. Then she looked up, a speculative gleam in her eyes. "I'm actually protected from pregnancy, if that's your main concern."

"You are?" His stomach fluttered with hope. He knew he didn't have any diseases, and he trusted her to be honest with him on that front.

She tilted her head to the side. "I have an IUD. So if you're okay with that…"

He started nodding before she even finished speaking. "Yes," he said emphatically. "I trust you."

Her smile was tender and full of understanding. "I trust you, too," she said quietly.

He tossed the condoms back into the drawer and rose to his feet. Without a word, he opened his arms. Rebecca walked forward until her chest pressed against his, her eyes locked on him. Moving slowly, Quinn lowered his head. He wanted to give her time to change her mind, even though it would kill him to let her go now.

He needn't have worried. As soon as their lips met, passion overtook them both. Rebecca's hands were everywhere, roaming over him, tugging at his clothes. He yanked up the hem of her shirt, needing to feel her skin. They both wanted access to each other's bodies, but neither wanted to break the kiss. After a few fumbling moments they managed to strip each other, then fell onto the bed, laughing at their clumsiness.

"I'm usually not so uncoordinated," she said, pulling him down for another kiss.

"No judgment here," he told her, coming up for air a moment later.

He'd meant to take his time, to go slowly as they explored each other and embarked on this new phase in their relationship. But his arousal quickly overwhelmed his self-control, and based on Rebecca's eager responses, her excitement matched his own.

Her hips moved restlessly against him, her desire clear. She placed her hands on his shoulders and rolled him over until he was flat on his back. Quinn was happy to let her take the lead; her obvious pleasure only served to heighten his own.

Rebecca threw a leg over his hips, straddling him. Their eyes met as she took him into her body, emotion arcing between them. A wave of tenderness filled him, his heart expanding until he thought it might burst in his chest. She was the woman for him, the one he needed in his life. He'd tried so hard to keep his distance, to guard his heart. But he didn't have the energy to protect himself any longer. As Rebecca moved over him, her expression was so open he felt he could see into her soul. This was more than just sex for her, too. They were both exposing themselves, opening their hearts to the possibility of love, of a life together.

Quinn didn't know how they would overcome the obstacles in their path. But as Rebecca smiled down at him, he didn't care. As long as she was with him, Quinn felt like he could take on the world.

Rebecca woke to find the room dark. Quinn was a warm weight against her back, his arm snug around her torso. His breath was hot against the nape of her neck, but she didn't mind.

She smiled as the memories of their encounter filled her thoughts. Her body twinged pleasantly from

Quinn's attentions, a delicious ache settling into her secret places.

Quinn had been a generous and attentive lover, bringing her pleasure before surrendering to his own needs. She'd felt cherished and treasured in his arms, as if she was something precious to him. Their encounter had been more than sex—she'd felt connected to Quinn both body and soul, as if their core selves had met and merged.

She searched her heart, half-expecting to find a kernel of guilt or regret. She hadn't felt this kind of overwhelming emotion since Brandon; was she betraying his memory by falling for another man?

No, she decided firmly. She wasn't. Brandon was dead, and while she'd always miss him, she had to go on living. Deep in her heart, she knew he would want her to move on. They'd truly loved each other—Brandon wouldn't want her to spend the rest of her life mourning a ghost. Falling for Quinn didn't diminish the love she'd felt for Brandon, or cheapen the bond they'd shared. Quinn was a different man, and her feelings for him had nothing to do with her past.

But what happened now?

The question of their future loomed large in her mind. She lived in Virginia and worked in DC—not exactly a short distance from Big Bend. She might be able to apply for a transfer to the El Paso office, but that was still several hours away from the park. Would Quinn be willing to consider relocating? There were several small parks in Maryland and Virginia.

It would be quite different from his time in Yosemite and Big Bend, but perhaps he'd be happy working at a smaller park if it meant they could be together.

Assuming that's what he wanted. Rebecca didn't think he was using her for sex—she could tell from the emotions she'd seen swirling in his eyes that last night had been special to him as well. But he might not be ready to commit to a relationship just yet. Given their past history of losses, it was possible he was gun-shy about diving in to something new.

He stirred, finding his way toward consciousness. They clearly had issues to discuss, but her worries could wait. For now, she intended to enjoy the moment.

For however long it lasted.

"I want to leave. Or I want my phone call." His eyes roamed around the room, reminding her of a tiger pacing a cage. He was edgy, that much was obvious. But why? Did he have something to hide?

"You're not under arrest," she said, hoping this news would help calm him. "I just want to talk for a little bit."

His eyes, small in his large face, landed on her. "Who are you?"

"Rebecca Wade. I'm with the FBI."

His face drained of color. "A fed?"

"Afraid so. Anything you want to tell me before we get started?"

He swallowed hard, his Adam's apple bobbing in his throat. He opened his mouth, then snapped it shut again and shook his head.

"Okay," she said easily. "Let's get to know each other, shall we? I see your name is Harrison Chambers, but your friends called you Harry. Can I call you Harry?"

He shrugged, the motion jerky.

Rebecca nodded. "Tell me how long you've been camping in Big Bend, Harry."

"Couple months, off and on," he said grudgingly.

"Do you live nearby?" According to his driver's license, he was a resident of Marfa, one of the small towns near the park.

"Yeah." He confirmed his address.

"But you prefer to camp in the park?"

"I live with my parents," he said. "The house is too small, and all they ever do is bitch at me."

"So the park is your refuge."

He frowned, clearly confused by her description. "I guess."

"And it's the same for your friends? They like to get out of the house, too?"

He nodded. "Yeah. It's better out there."

She imagined it was. None of the young men had a job, and it sounded like their parents were tired of supporting their aimless lifestyles. It made sense they would chafe at the constant reminders of their failures. Camping in the park was their sanctuary, their escape from the reality of their disappointing lives.

"What do you guys like to do while you camp?" Hiking the trails was probably not on their agenda, if Harry's physical condition was any indication.

He looked at her like she was crazy. "The usual stuff," he said. "Hanging out."

"Drinking and smoking?" she offered.

Harry shrugged, as if that should be obvious. She pictured it easily; three young men, drinking and smoking every night until the early hours of the morning, then sleeping late the next day as they tried to recover.

"Tell me about your encounters with Park Ranger Gallagher."

Harry narrowed his eyes. "The guy's a jerk." He launched into a tirade against Quinn, his anger building as he spoke. It was clear Harry hated Quinn—

unless she missed her guess, Rebecca figured Harry saw Quinn as the embodiment of all that was wrong with his world. What had started out as a chance encounter when Quinn had enforced park rules had turned into a near obsession for the young man. Quinn was the reason he couldn't get a job. Quinn was the one keeping him from being successful in life. It was Quinn's fault Harry didn't have a girl-friend. The list of grievances went on and on, and Harry grew more and more agitated with every word.

She understood his jealousy—Quinn was Harry's opposite in practically every way. Harry seemed in-capable of accepting responsibility for his own poor choices, so he projected blame onto Quinn, building the ranger up in his mind as his enemy.

Rebecca nodded with false sympathy the whole time, listening attentively as Harry spoke. "He sounds pretty awful," she said. "Do you ever think about get-ting back at him for all the trouble he's caused you?"

"Oh, yeah." Harry's grin was full of malice. "He needs to be put in his place."

"What do you want to do to him?"

Harry formed a fist with his left hand and pounded it gently against his right palm. "Let's just say, if I found him in a dark alley, I'd give him a nice tune-up."

"Given the way he talks to you, I'm surprised you haven't done it already."

"Oh, I want to," Harry assured her. "But he's the kind of wimp that would press charges. He's not worth the jail time."

So Harry did have a bit of self-control where his anger was concerned. But Rebecca read between the lines; he wasn't averse to violence, he just didn't want to get caught and deal with the punishment.

"Do you have a girlfriend?" She already knew the answer, but she wanted to see Harry's reaction to the question.

"No." His tone was a bit sullen, as if he was unhappy about his lack of a love life.

"What about your friends? Any of them have someone special?"

Harry shook his head. "We don't have time for that kind of drama."

Rebecca nodded, pretending to understand. "Better off single, am I right?"

"Yeah."

But it was clear Harry wasn't happy about the status quo. This young man was stewing in a toxic mix of emotions—anger and frustration toward Quinn, longing for women who rejected him and a general dissatisfaction with his life. Had something finally caused him to snap?

Rebecca opened the file she'd brought in with her and carefully withdrew the pictures of the victims. She placed the first one in front of Harry.

"Do you recognize this woman?"

Harry glanced at the photo. "No. But she's kinda hot."

Rebecca's stomach turned, but she kept her reaction hidden as she put the second photo on the table. "What about this one?"

Harry shook his head. Rebecca added the third photo. "I don't know any of these chicks," Harry said. He studied the pictures for a moment. "Wait, are they dead?" A strange note entered his voice—part excitement, part revulsion. A chill skittered down Rebecca's spine at his reaction. Most people were distressed by the sight of a corpse. But Harry seemed to find it titillating…

"How did they die?" He glanced up, his eyes bright. It was exactly the kind of response a killer might have when looking at the evidence of his work. Rebecca's heart thudded in her chest. Had she found the murderer?

"How do you think they died?" The photos showed only the women's faces, nothing more. There was no way to tell cause of death from the cropped shots, so Harry's response would be telling.

He stared at the pictures, his breathing quickening a bit as he glanced from victim to victim. *He's not touching the photos*, Rebecca realized with a jolt. Harry was completely absorbed by the pictures, but he was being very careful not to actually touch them as he turned from one to the other. *Afraid of leaving fingerprints?* she wondered. So far, the forensic evidence at each site had been depressingly lacking. The killer was clearly taking pains to cover his tracks, and Harry's abnormal display of caution was a red flag.

"I think they were stabbed," he said finally, smiling a little at the thought.

"What makes you say that?" Either he really wasn't the killer, or he was pretending he didn't know anything about the murders to deflect suspicion.

Harry jerked one shoulder up in a careless shrug. "Look at them. All pretty, and you could tell they knew it. Probably teased the wrong guy one too many times."

"You think he simply snapped?" That didn't fit the killer's careful behavior, but she wanted to see where Harry was going with this. How elaborate was his story going to be?

"Probably. Can you blame him? Women like that…" He trailed off, shaking his head.

"Got what they deserved?" she suggested.

Harry shrugged again as if to suggest "what more could you expect?"

"Maybe you're right." Rebecca swept up the photos and returned them to the folder.

"I am," he said confidently. "You'll see." He shifted in the chair, then frowned slightly. "Say, why did you show me those pictures anyway?"

About time you asked, Rebecca thought. "The women were all found dead in Big Bend Park. I was wondering if you'd seen them around while you and your buddies were camping."

"Oh." He sounded a little disappointed and his expression grew thoughtful. *Reliving the event?* she wondered.

Truth be told, she wasn't sure Harry was smart enough to kill three women without leaving evidence behind. Furthermore, his two buddies weren't exactly criminal masterminds, either. It was possible Harry had acted on his own, but his friends likely would have noticed his absence.

Still, killer or no, this young man was dangerous. Unfortunately, Rebecca couldn't keep him in custody any longer. There simply wasn't enough evidence, and her gut feeling that he was a bad kid wasn't sufficient justification for detaining him.

She pushed to her feet, file folder in hand. Harry stood when she opened the door, jamming his hands in his pockets.

"Thank you for your time. You're free to go."

"That's it?" Relief tinged his voice and Rebecca clenched her jaw. Was she letting the killer slip through her fingers?

"For now," she said. "But I might need to talk to you again, so please stay in the area."

He grinned. "Sure thing. Got a full moon coming up in a few days. Wouldn't want to miss seeing it." He looked her up and down with a leer. "You should camp with me some time. It's amazing what you can see at night away from the city lights."

Rebecca's skin crawled and she fought the urge to vomit. "I'm sure it's quite pretty."

"Think about it," Harry said, sauntering past her. He took his hands out of his pockets, and a small white object dropped to the floor. Rebecca opened her mouth to say something out of habit, but snapped it shut again and watched him walk away. After Harry turned the corner, she walked over and kneeled down to study his lost item.

Nothing but a joint, she realized with disappointment. Maybe that was why he'd seemed so nervous upon hearing she worked for the FBI—he probably thought she was going to bust him for possession. It wasn't the kind of evidence she needed to tie him to three murders. But perhaps still helpful?

She flagged down an officer and instructed him to bag the evidence and send it to the lab. They might be able to retrieve DNA and fingerprints from the crudely rolled cigarette. It would be good to have Harry's information on file.

Something about his parting remarks rankled her. Why had he mentioned the upcoming full moon? She had caught a few killers who attached special significance to astrological occurrences. Was he taunting her with the promise of another victim soon? It was a possibility she couldn't ignore. There was no astrological significance attached to the murder dates of the first three victims, but perhaps he was evolving. The third woman had been killed only five days after the second, rather than the expected week. What else was changing?

Ten minutes and two phone calls later, she climbed into her car with a sigh of disgust. She'd asked the police to keep a watchful eye on Harry and his friends, but they'd made it clear they lacked the man power to follow three kids on the off chance they might do something. She'd already requested additional resources to assist in the investigation, but the wheels turned slowly and even a couple of phone calls hadn't been enough to speed things up. It would be a few days before more officers arrived to help, and in the meantime, the young men could disappear.

Rebecca wasn't convinced Harry was the killer, but she didn't think he was entirely innocent, either. She'd just have to dig a little deeper to discover what kind of skeletons he had in his closet.

Quinn glanced at the door for what had to be the millionth time, hoping to catch sight of Rebecca coming in to the ranger station. He'd been thinking about her all morning, but not just because of last night. She was talking to the three troublemakers this morning, and he was dying to know how the interviews had gone.

Maybe this is the break she needs to crack the case. The thought she might be with the killer now made him want to rush to her side to protect her, even though he knew she was perfectly safe. They were in the local police station, surrounded by officers. What could possibly happen?

Part of him wished desperately the young men were responsible for the murders—if they were in custody, women would stop dying. But if the killer or killers had been apprehended, Rebecca would be leaving soon. A selfish corner of his heart wasn't ready for that yet.

Last night had been amazing. He hadn't felt that kind of connection with another person since Ashley's death. It wasn't just the sex, although that had been enjoyable in its own right. He'd bared his soul to Rebecca last night, and he knew she'd done the same with him. They'd faced each other, naked in every possible way. It had both humbled and thrilled him to receive the gift of her vulnerability—he knew she didn't lower her guard for just anyone, and the fact that she'd shown him her heart last night meant she must have feelings for him.

He was certainly falling in love with her.

The knowledge settled over him, spreading across his heart and mind in a slow crawl. He pondered the realization, half-afraid of the emotions that might flare up in response to this development. *What about Ashley?* he wondered. He had deliberately ignored the memories of his wife last night, but now he had to wonder if he was doing the right thing. It wasn't the idea of love that scared him—he knew Ashley would have wanted him to move on with his life. But was it all too much, too soon?

Rebecca was a special woman—he'd known that from the start. But was he letting his fascination with her blind him to the risks of falling in love?

He didn't think she'd deliberately hurt him—she wasn't cruel. Still, he couldn't ignore the fact that he lived and worked in Texas, while she called Virginia home. It wasn't a stretch to imagine the distance of thousands of miles would make a relationship difficult, if not impossible. And she probably wasn't interested in moving here…

Quinn shook his head, dismissing the thought. *Getting ahead of yourself, there.* Just because they'd slept together didn't mean he needed to worry about rearranging his life, or ask her to do the same. Talk about putting the cart before the horse!

He didn't even know how Rebecca was feeling, now that she'd had time to process things. When he'd driven her back to her car this morning, things had been pleasant and easygoing between them, with no hint of tension or regret. But it was possible she was now having second thoughts, or perhaps their encounter hadn't affected her the way it had rocked him. There were a lot of unknown variables to consider, and until they spoke again, he was wasting his time and energy worrying about things he couldn't change.

A chime sounded in the office, indicating a visitor to the center. He leaned back in his chair to get a view of the door, hoping it was her…

It was. Rebecca strode into the lobby and made a beeline for the counter, skirting past the ranger on desk duty with a nod. Quinn studied her face as she approached. She didn't look particularly happy—there was a small furrow between her eyebrows, and the corners of her mouth were turned down in a frown.

Quinn stood, filled with determination. He didn't know what had made her upset, but he wanted to fix it.

She gave him a fleeting smile as she approached. "Hey," she said.

He wanted to reach for her, to draw her close and kiss her. But he wasn't sure how she'd respond to such a public display in front of everyone, so he settled for a smile. "You don't look happy."

She dropped into the chair across from his desk with a sigh. "I talked to Harry and his friends this morning." She shook her head. "Two of them seem okay, but Harry is dangerous."

Quinn sat up straight. "Did he try to hurt you?" He'd assumed that because she was talking to him in the police station she'd be safe, but maybe he should have gone with her after all…

Rebecca shook her head. "No. But it's clear that he's headed down a bad path."

"So you don't think he's the killer?"

"I'm not sure," she said thoughtfully. "There are aspects of his behavior that have me worried, but nothing that definitively ties him to the victims. Of course, this was just the initial interview. It's possible if I spoke to him again, he'd reveal something more conclusive."

"I take it you had to let him go?"

She nodded, her expression sour. "I couldn't hold him any longer. And I spoke with the police chief— they don't have the resources to follow the guys and keep tabs on them. My reinforcements aren't due to arrive for another couple of days, so until we get more man power, Harry and his friends are free to roam the park."

"You think they might disappear?" Quinn wasn't entirely bothered by the thought, but he knew wherever the group members went, they'd cause trouble. Probably better to deal with them here, rather than pass the buck off to some unsuspecting community.

"It's possible." She tucked a strand of hair behind her ear. Quinn was suddenly overcome by the sense memory of her hair trailing across his stomach as she moved down his body… Goose bumps broke out along his skin and he shivered a bit, trying to shake off the distraction.

"I'm worried that we tipped our hand," she continued, apparently oblivious to Quinn's reaction. "Now that they know we're interested in them, they'll either leave or change their behavior so we don't catch them doing something wrong."

"Maybe that's not a bad thing," he pointed out, trying to put his brain back on track. "Not the disappearing part. But if they start behaving themselves, that's a good outcome, right?"

"To a point," she conceded. "I've worked cases like this before, where the main suspect acted like a pillar of the community once he realized we were watching."

"What happened?" If Rebecca's expression was anything to go by, the situation hadn't ended well.

She glanced down. "He faked being a good guy for so long, the police couldn't justify keeping him under sustained surveillance. After a few months, he went back to his old ways and killed three more people before he was arrested."

"Oh." Quinn's stomach sank. "So if Harry really is the killer, this could make things worse?"

"That's what I'm afraid of," she confirmed. Her expression turned thoughtful. "I just don't know if he's the murderer. He definitely has the capacity for violence, and a disturbing interest in hurting women."

A wave of revulsion washed over Quinn. "But?" he asked.

Rebecca shook her head slowly. "But…he appears to lack the discipline and impulse control displayed by the Yoga Killer. Harry is a hothead who is ruled by emotion. The Yoga Killer is methodical and cool, not someone who can be provoked into making a mistake."

"Maybe Harry can focus when he needs to."

"Maybe." But she sounded unsure, and Quinn didn't think it was a likely possibility, either. In all his dealings with Harry and his friends, the young man had always come across as brash and imma-ture, the kind of guy who hit first and asked ques-tions later. He didn't doubt Rebecca's assessment of Harry's potential for violence, but the young man wasn't exactly a planner.

"You think he's more of a crime-of-opportunity kind of guy?" he suggested. It fit what he knew of Harry's personality—immediate gratification, no thought required.

"Exactly." Rebecca smiled at him, looking like a

proud teacher. "But until I can definitively rule him out, I want to keep an eye on him."

"Why do I get the feeling you're planning something?"

She looked at him with wide eyes, the very picture of innocence. But he wasn't fooled. "Who, me?"

"R-eebec-ca," he said, drawing out her name a bit. "Come on. Spill it."

She dropped the act. "I can't let these guys go unsupervised. Not until I know more. I'm going to have to watch them myself."

Her declaration set off alarm bells in Quinn's head. The plan sounded terrible to him. Not only did she lack experience in camping, but she also didn't need to be anywhere near those young men. Especially not with the remoteness of the park, where help was hours away...

"No," he said automatically. "That's not a good idea."

She gave him a cool look, one eyebrow arched. "I wasn't asking for your permission."

Quinn closed his eyes and sighed quietly, digging deep for patience. Didn't she see he wasn't trying to control her or tell her what to do? He was simply concerned for her safety and wanted her to see reason. He understood the impulse to do *something*, but that didn't mean she needed to throw caution to the wind and act recklessly.

"I didn't think you were," he said evenly. "But I'm not going to stay quiet and let you put yourself in danger just because you're frustrated by the lack of resources right now. You don't know the first thing about camping, and you certainly don't need to learn on the fly while trying to monitor the actions of three volatile young men who may or may not be killers. Not to mention, their campsite is a bit off the beaten path, so you'd be far from help if anything went wrong."

She waved her hand carelessly, brushing aside his concerns. "I figured that out already. But you don't need to worry."

"Why's that?" He had a sinking suspicion he knew what she was about to say next.

"I won't be alone. You're coming with me."

"I see. I suppose I should be glad to hear there's room for me in your plan." He couldn't keep the sarcasm from his voice, but Rebecca didn't seem to notice.

"Naturally."

"I still think this is a bad idea." Even though they'd have to set up camp a few miles away from the men, Quinn still didn't like the thought of being so close to them. Now that they'd been questioned by Rebecca, they had to know something was going on. Was it enough to make them desperate? To make them even more reckless than usual? If they somehow stumbled across Quinn and Rebecca, there was no telling how they'd respond. And with help so far away, he and Rebecca were practically asking for trouble.

The whole situation left him with a bad taste in his mouth, but he could tell by Rebecca's determined expression she wasn't going to accept no for an answer. A small part of him admired her tenacity even as frustration filled him.

"Is there anything I can say to get you to change your mind?"

"No." She shook her head. "But your concerns are noted." She leaned forward and put her hand over his. "I don't want to be stupid about this, Quinn. But I can't leave these guys alone until I'm sure they're not involved. I'd never forgive myself if I turned a blind eye and they hurt someone else."

He nodded grudgingly, understanding the impulse. His desire to catch the killer matched her own, and if she thought this was going to help, who was he to argue with the expert?

"Okay," he said. "I'll help you. But we do this my way, understood? We're not going to get too close to their campsite, and we're only going to observe."

She smiled at him. "Whatever you say. I trust you."

Those three little words struck him in the heart like an arrow, piercing the last of his resistance. "I suppose you want to set up camp today?" He reached for a notepad and pen, already running down a list of the supplies they'd need to bring...

"Yes. The sooner, the better. If you tell me what food we'll need, I can run to the grocery store while you get the other stuff ready."

He sent her off with a list a few minutes later. She left quickly, clearly eager to get started.

Quinn watched her leave, unable to shake his unease. Rebecca's plan made sense, and he understood her motivations for insisting on the surveillance. But Harry and his friends were nothing if not unpredictable, and Quinn couldn't help but worry over what they might do if they discovered they were being watched.

He typed out an email to his supervisor, explaining the outline of Rebecca's plan and giving their general expected location, should anything happen. It made him feel a little better to know his coworkers would be aware of their whereabouts, should anything happen.

Quinn turned his attention back to the list, silently debating. He had a pistol at home, tucked away in a closet. It was on the older side, but he kept up with the maintenance and it should work if necessary. Guns weren't allowed in the park, but if ever there was time for an exception to be made…

He pulled out his wallet, checking to make sure his gun permit was still there. If he was going to do something illegal, he'd best have all his other ducks in a row.

His mind made up, Quinn grabbed his keys and headed for the door. Rebecca was going to meet him at his apartment with the groceries, and he wanted to have all the other supplies ready when she arrived. It was late in the day to start a camping trip, and he didn't want to get caught on the trail when darkness fell.

"It'll be fine," he told himself as he drove home. "Nothing to get worked up about."

But no matter how many times he said it, he still heard the voice of doubt in his mind.

Chapter 11

"This is a good spot."

Rebecca dropped her pack to the ground with a sigh of relief and rolled her aching shoulders. They'd been hiking for almost two hours, and with all the supplies they needed, her bag was much heavier than she was used to.

She glanced over at Quinn, who had removed his bag and was methodically sorting the pieces of the tent. He'd had a much heavier load to carry, but he hadn't complained once. She knew he wasn't crazy about this idea, but she appreciated his going along with it nonetheless.

"You should drink something," he said, eyes still on his task. "It was a tough climb."

Rebecca nodded and sat, pulling out a water bottle from her bag. She took a long draw and offered it to Quinn. He hesitated for a second, then accepted it with a shrug.

"Where are they?" she said, craning her neck to scan the landscape. "I don't see their camp at all."

Quinn jerked his head to the left. "Down by that tree, about two hundred yards away."

She squinted in that direction, finally finding the spot. "Oh," she said, a little disappointed. "Can't we get closer?"

"No." Quinn's tone was final—he was clearly not in the mood to debate this point. He passed over a pair of high-powered binoculars, and just like that, the campsite came into clear focus. "This is as close as we need to get to them."

"Okay." Looking through the binoculars, Rebecca had to admit Quinn had chosen a good spot for their site. They were on a wide, flat section on the side of the mountain, giving them the high ground. The slope of the land and the large boulders nearby provided some measure of shade, which would be invaluable tomorrow during the heat of the day. Most importantly, though, Quinn was setting up the site so the mountain was at their back. No one would be able to sneak up on them. From this vantage point, she could watch Harry and his friends all day without having to worry about danger approaching from behind.

It didn't take long for Quinn to set up the tent. Rebecca offered to help, but it was clear he knew what he was doing and her clumsy attempts at assistance only slowed him down. So she contented herself with organizing the rest of their supplies and setting up the two camping chairs they'd brought.

The sun was starting to set by the time the tent was in place. Quinn unrolled their sleeping bags inside, then stepped out of the tent to join her.

Rebecca gave him an absent smile as he settled into the chair next to her. She was unable to tear her gaze from the sky, mesmerized by the fiery display as the sun sank toward the horizon. Shades of orange and yellow and peach melted into one another, a desert kaleidoscope that was breathtaking in intensity and scope. The colors were so vibrant it almost hurt to look at them, but she persisted. She'd never seen anything like this before in Virginia—it was like stepping onto another planet.

Quinn moved unobtrusively next to her, busying himself with some task. She knew she should offer to help, but the sky was changing before her eyes and she couldn't bear to miss any of it. Finally, as the red sky began to morph into shades of violet and purple, she turned away.

Quinn met her eyes and smiled in understanding. "It's pretty amazing, isn't it?"

"Stunning. I've never seen colors like that before."

He nodded. "Was that the first time you've ever stopped to watch the sun set?"

It was a simple question, and yet it hit her with the force of a blow. Quinn was right—how many times had she worked until dark, never stopping to appreciate the natural beauty around her? How many moments had she missed simply because she hadn't bothered to look?

She blinked hard as tears stung her eyes. Brandon had never been one to slow down, and consequently, neither had she. She'd fallen into the habit of wearing blinders, of focusing solely on what was in front of her. But being with Quinn had widened her gaze. Even in the middle of this investigation, she'd enjoyed herself and the time they spent together. Who knew something as simple as a desert sunset could be so magical?

He reached out to gently touch her cheek. "I'm glad you got to see it," he said softly. His eyes were warm with affection, drawing her in.

She leaned over and pressed a soft kiss to his mouth, wanting that connection. "Me, too," she said.

"There's more to come," he said. "The night sky is pretty amazing, and sunrise is hard to beat as well." He passed her a sandwich on a plate. "You might get so caught up in the natural world you forget to spy on those boys."

"I wish," she said ruefully. It would be nice to focus only on the beauty of her surroundings, but she did have a job to do. Still, that didn't mean she couldn't enjoy herself while she was there…

"Thank you for this," she said, between bites of her sandwich.

Quinn shrugged. "It's not much, but since we can't build a fire it'll have to do."

"No, I meant thank you for doing this with me. I know you don't think it's a good idea."

He sighed softly and poked at a few chips with his forefinger. "I just want you to be safe. Is that such a bad thing?"

"Of course not," Rebecca replied. "And I do appreciate your concern. But in this case, the danger is minimal. Watchful waiting is the name of the game."

"Hopefully, they'll be too drunk to notice us," Quinn said darkly. "Because otherwise, I don't think they'd take too kindly to our presence."

"Probably not," she replied. But she wasn't worried. Unbeknownst to Quinn, she had brought her service revolver and she knew how to use it. She'd never fired at an actual person before, but if she had to protect herself or Quinn, she wouldn't hesitate.

She finished her food and washed it down with the last of the water from the bottle. Then she stood, gathering up her trash. "So what's going to pass for facilities while we're here?"

Quinn tilted his head to the left. "Head back down the trail about twenty feet. There's a cluster of boulders you can use for privacy."

"Oh." She'd known there would be no true bathrooms around, but now that she was faced with the reality of the situation, the prospect of roughing it was decidedly unappealing.

Quinn's mouth twitched with a knowing smile.

"Having second thoughts? It's not too late to go back to the land of flushing toilets, sinks and hot showers." He dangled the words in front of her like a salesman hawking his wares, and for a moment, she was sorely tempted. But determination stiffened her spine and made her shake her head. She was a professional, and she wasn't about to let a little thing like peeing outside keep her from doing her job.

"I'll be fine," she said, putting on a brave face.

"I'm sure you will," Quinn said, amusement lacing his tone. He handed her a small bag.

"What's this?" She peeked inside to see a spade, a roll of toilet paper and a bottle of hand sanitizer.

"Your toiletries kit," he said. "The toilet paper is specially made to degrade quickly. Use the spade to dig a hole, take care of your business, then cover it up. No one will ever know you were there."

"I see," she said. "You thought of everything, didn't you?"

He grinned openly now, clearly enjoying her discomfort. "Not my first rodeo, princess."

Rebecca's cheeks warmed. "Thank you," she said stiffly.

Quinn bowed elaborately, then began to clean up their meal. "Off you go."

She shoved her empty plate and water bottle into a bag and spun on her heel, heading off with as much dignity as she could muster. It took a few minutes to find a suitable spot, and a few more to do what needed to be done. Finally, though, she headed back toward their camp in possession of a newly acquired skill she'd never thought she'd need.

There was a bright glow from the direction of Harry's camp, and she realized they had lit a fire. *Good*, she thought grimly. Quinn wouldn't be happy to see that, but it would help her keep an eye on them tonight.

She rounded the last bend in the trail, expecting to see Quinn staring down at the illegal campfire with his hands on his hips. But the site was empty.

"Quinn?" She poked her head into the tent, searching for him. Her voice echoed faintly off the surrounding rocks. She winced at the sound, not wanting to alert Harry or his friends to their presence. She grabbed the binoculars and took a quick look at their site; two young men were sitting around the fire, drinking beer and laughing. They showed no sign of having heard her call. She frowned, studying them carefully. Where was Harry?

She lowered her voice. "Quinn?" she asked again. She walked to the edge of the campsite, peering into the growing darkness. *He's probably using the bathroom*, she told herself, trying to squelch the sense of unease rising in her belly. *He'll be back soon.*

But she couldn't shake the feeling that something was wrong. Where was Harry? Why wasn't he sitting around the fire, drinking with his friends? She'd seen him earlier, when she'd taken her first look at their camp. His absence now was glaring, and even though it was probably just a coincidence, she couldn't help but feel worried about Quinn's unexplained disappearance as well.

Rebecca forced herself to sit in one of the chairs, the binoculars glued to her eyes as she spied on the young men. She told herself she was simply being paranoid, but as the minutes ticked by with no sign of either Quinn or Harry, she knew in her bones something was wrong. She glanced at her phone, cursing softly as she saw the device showed no service available.

Finally, she could stand it no longer. She pushed to her feet, grabbing a flashlight from her bag. Then she pulled her gun from its ankle holster and checked to make sure the safety was on. She was already feeling jumpy; the last thing she needed was to accidentally shoot herself if something startled her.

She hadn't encountered Quinn on her way back to the camp, which meant he had gone in the opposite direction. Gathering up her courage, Rebecca set off down the trail, leaving behind the illusion of safety as she headed into the purple darkness.

Quinn had been watching Rebecca head down the trail, admiring her graceful movements as she headed for her makeshift bathroom. He'd chuckled softly at her reaction to the toiletry kit he'd given her—it was clear she was out of her element, and yet she was determined to see this through to the end. Admiration had welled in his chest; it was hard to hold on to his frustration in the face of her dedication to what she thought was right.

It didn't take long to clean up after their simple dinner. Quinn glanced at the sky, the last sliver of the sun just beginning to disappear over the horizon. It would be full dark soon. He should probably make his own bathroom trip before night set in.

He rummaged in his bag for the other kit, then headed off down the trail in the opposite direction Rebecca had taken. He moved easily across the loose stones in the path, his eyes adjusting to the growing darkness as he walked. This was his favorite time of day when camping—the transition between daylight and night, when everything was quiet and the world seemed to take a breath before the nocturnal animals woke and began their evening activities. The first stars would begin to appear soon, dotting the sky like diamonds strewn across velvet. It was a view that never failed to take his breath away.

He finished up and took a moment to look at the moon. It was waxing toward full, putting out a soft, luminous glow that would bathe the campsite in silver light. Under any other circumstances, it would have made things romantic. But he knew they were here to do a job, and even though he wouldn't mind getting his hands on Rebecca again, he didn't think a sleeping bag and tent would provide the right kind of ambience for her.

Too bad.

With a shake of his head, Quinn started to walk back toward camp. He'd gone only a few steps when he heard a soft rustle behind him. The hairs on the back of his neck stood on end, and he had the distinct sensation he was being watched. He glanced behind him, but saw nothing.

Probably just an animal, he thought. Hopefully, not a mountain lion on the hunt; he was easy pickings for a big cat, alone and defenseless on the trail. He'd left his gun in his pack, not thinking to bring it along on such a pedestrian trip. Maybe that had been a mistake...

He quickened his steps a bit, eager to make it back to camp. The rustling sound followed him, getting louder this time. Quinn's stomach sank and his heart began to race as he realized he was being followed. Why had he left the gun back at camp? It was a stupid oversight, one that might cost him dearly. Determined to find something to defend himself with, he thrust his hand into the bag he carried and withdrew the spade. It wasn't much, but if he had to fight back, it was better than nothing.

He kept moving, pretending to ignore the sounds behind him. Then, without warning, he whirled with a shout, the spade lifted high in defense.

He'd expected to find an animal on the trail—a wild pig, or perhaps a young cougar. Instead, he saw a man a few steps behind, his features obscured by a dark bandanna.

Quinn stumbled back a step, his mind racing. Who was this, and why were they following him? He hadn't seen anyone else on the trail today, so where had this guy come from?

He lowered the spade, uncertainty setting in. He couldn't very well attack a man for walking behind him. But then Quinn saw the flash of metal in the darkness and realized his mistake. The man had a knife, and it looked like he wanted to use it.

Quinn took another step back, trying to maintain distance between them. "I'm not looking for any trouble," he said. He tightened his grip on the spade, his muscles tensing in anticipation. The man didn't reply, but continued to approach. Quinn planted his feet, refusing to give any more ground. Rebecca might be back at the camp by now—he wasn't about to lead this man to her and risk her safety as well.

"What do you want?" Quinn challenged. He squinted, trying to determine the color of the man's eyes. "I'm not afraid of you, Harry," he said, throwing out the name on a guess. Had the young man realized he and his friends were being watched? Perhaps he'd come to intimidate them into leaving.

The man stopped a few feet away, still silent. He looked a little smaller than what Quinn remembered of Harry, but maybe the kid had lost weight? His loose layers of clothes made it difficult to really gauge his build. Quinn shifted his weight to the balls of his feet, ready to move. "Go back to your friends," he said, jerking his head in the direction of their camp, but never taking his eyes off Harry. "I'm sure they're missing you by now."

The stranger cocked his head to the side, as if considering the possibility. Then he lunged forward, knife extended, quick as a striking snake. Quinn barely had time to jerk out of the way, but the knife still found him. A searing line of pain bisected the side of his ribs, and he realized with a sense of shock that he'd been cut.

He yelped and thrust blindly. The man let out a grunt as the tip of the spade made contact with his flesh, but it wasn't enough to slow him down. He struck again, this time slicing across Quinn's shoulder blades.

Quinn kicked out, aiming for the man's knee. He realized with a growing sense of desperation that his only chance was to hobble the man so he could get away. The spade simply wasn't going to be enough of a weapon in the face of the knife.

The assailant dodged his first kick, but Quinn got lucky the second time and landed a glancing blow that set the stranger stumbling back a few steps. Quinn pressed his temporary advantage, advancing quickly to stab at the man with the point of the spade. He drew blood, but it wasn't enough. Another swing of the knife connected with Quinn's chest, and he jerked away, out of range.

Quinn's shirt clung to his skin, wet and sticky, as the blood saturating the fabric began to cool. His heart raced in his chest and his tongue felt thick in his mouth. His head began to swim, but he stubbornly clung to consciousness. If he passed out, he was dead.

He stood in the middle of the path, swaying slightly as he and the stranger stared at each other. The man was bleeding freely from Quinn's earlier attack, but he didn't seem bothered by his injuries, at least not in Quinn's fuzzy view. He eyed Quinn up and down, as if assessing his chances of another successful attack. Apparently, the stranger liked what he saw. He tightened his grip on the knife and stepped forward.

Quinn planted his feet, knowing this was his last chance. He had to make it count.

He was so focused on the man in front of him, he didn't hear anything else. Then suddenly a woman's voice rang out behind him and the scene was flooded with light.

"Freeze!"

The stranger jerked to a stop, apparently just as startled at the intrusion. He squinted at the unexpected illumination, throwing up a hand to shield his eyes. Quinn took advantage of his confusion to strike again, this time making contact with the man's forearm. The stranger grunted and lashed out, landing another blow with his knife. Quinn yelped in pain, trying to retreat out of the man's reach. The stranger stepped forward, his knife raised to deliver the killing blow.

A thunderous boom split the air, and Quinn felt a gust of wind pass by his arm. The man froze, then turned and ran, bounding down the trail like a gazelle.

Quinn dropped to his knees, gasping for breath. Everything hurt—his body felt shredded and raw, throbbing with pain like an exposed nerve ending.

But he couldn't afford to let down his guard. The man was gone now, but he'd be back.

He felt a hand on his shoulder and turned to see Rebecca's face, worry etched in the lines of her frown. "My God," she whispered, running her gaze over him. "What happened?"

Quinn tried to respond but could only shake his head. He was still trying to figure that out for himself.

"Never mind," she said. She rose to her feet and tugged on his arm. "We can't stay here. Let's get you back to camp so I can take a look at you."

He found his voice. "No," he said, the word jagged and harsh. "Too dangerous. We have to move."

"You're not in any condition—"

"There are small caves in the mountain," he interrupted. "We need to find one and hide until help arrives." He fumbled for the radio clipped to his belt, pulling it free. Rebecca could contact the ranger station and let them know what had happened. They'd have to spend a few hours out here alone, but as long as they could hide, they should be okay until reinforcements arrived.

He passed her the radio as they moved down the trail, back toward their supplies. She kept her arm around him as they walked, supporting him as he lurched along. Every step was exhausting, but Quinn knew he couldn't afford to give up now. Rebecca was strong, but there was no way she could drag his limp body to safety. And since she was too stubborn to leave him if he passed out, his only option was to keep moving forward.

It seemed to take an eternity, but they finally made it back to the tent. Quinn collapsed into one of the folding chairs, his muscles giving out after the exertion of the walk. "The supplies," he said, his voice shaky to his own ears. "Get the bags." It wouldn't take Rebecca long to gather their two packs of supplies. They'd need all the food and water while they waited for help, and there was a small medical kit in his backpack that she could hopefully use to stop his bleeding. His head swam as he watched her move in the moonlight. Her face was tight with worry and fear, but she didn't fall apart. She gathered their supplies, slinging one pack onto her back and strapping the other to her chest. Quinn felt a spurt of pride at her actions—if he had to deal with mystery attackers in the wilds of Big Bend, there was no better person to have by his side. A strange sense of calm fell over him as she approached, determination shining in her eyes. He was hurt badly, but he knew Rebecca would take care of him. If there was anyone who could handle this emergency, it was her.

"Let's get moving," she said. She bent forward, draping one of his arms across her shoulders. Then she stood, pulling him up out of the chair. He helped her as much as he could, but he could tell from the soft "oomph" she let out that his weight was heavy for her.

"Take the packs first," he suggested. She could

find a place for them to hide with the supplies, then come back for him.

"No," she said simply. He couldn't see her face, but he imagined her expression was determined.

He sighed, knowing it was pointless to argue with her. Better to save his energy for the walk ahead.

Her hand found the slice across his ribs, sending a fresh jolt of pain through his body. His breath caught in his throat, but he didn't complain. If anything, the pressure of her touch would help slow the bleeding.

"Which way?"

He nodded south, toward the path they'd used earlier to arrive at this site. "There's a small fork in the trail about thirty yards back. We'll take it and head farther up the mountain. I know of a small cave not far off." Hopefully, he could make it there...

Rebecca didn't reply. He felt her chest rise as she took a deep breath, and the two of them set out into the darkness together.

Chapter 12

Keep moving. Just keep moving.

Rebecca silently repeated the mantra as she and Quinn half walked and half stumbled up the trail. She didn't know how badly he was hurt, but his shirt was wet underneath her hand and the coppery tang of blood filled her nostrils and coated her tongue, making her want to gag. Quinn's breath was a series of harsh gusts against her ear, and she wondered how much farther he could go. He'd said the caves were close, but could they make it there before he collapsed?

"Almost...there," he gasped, as if he'd read her thoughts. She didn't know if he was trying to reassure her or himself. Either way, his words gave her a jolt of hope. Ignoring the burning protest of her muscles, she pushed on, running off a potent cocktail of adrenaline and fear.

Quinn gave her directions, guiding her off the path and across a rocky stretch of terrain. It was rough going, but they took their time. Quinn's determination was an almost palpable support, propelling him forward. Neither one of them acknowledged the silent truth—if he fell now, he might never get back up.

The thought sent a jolt of fear down Rebecca's spine, and she tightened her grip on his side. He grunted softly. "Sorry," she whispered, realizing she'd hurt him.

He didn't respond, but gave her shoulder a gentle squeeze of acknowledgment. She glanced at the wall of rock to their left, peering in the darkness for any signs they might be getting close to the cave Quinn had in mind. The mountain was a study of shadows, with overhanging rocks and stubby trees and bushes casting dark patches across the uneven surface. She spied some small, narrow entrances and her imagination took off, picturing sharp teeth and bright eyes watching as she and Quinn hobbled past. A sharp, high scream pierced the air, sending her heart into her throat and making her jump.

"Mountain lion," Quinn said, confirming her worries. An instinctive, bone-deep terror gripped Rebecca as she realized they were in danger of becoming prey. Never before had she questioned her position on the food chain, but here in the dark, with the smell of blood thick in the air and the call of a predator echoing in her ears, she felt a primitive fear that made all the hairs on her body stand on end.

"She's not that close," Quinn said, apparently recognizing her reaction. "But we don't need to linger." His words were labored—it was clear he would soon be out of energy.

"Save your breath," she advised. She needed Quinn to stay conscious for as long as possible. Not just to guide her to the cave, but to instruct her on how to survive the rest of the night. Once they'd arrived at a safe place, she would call for help. But it would take a while for anyone to find them, and she didn't want to pass the time alone. Talking to Quinn, even if just about silly little things, would help keep her calm while they waited.

After what seemed like an eternity, Quinn pointed at a large shadow ahead. "Just there," he said. Rebecca squinted at it, but saw nothing unusual about this spot—it looked like any of the other millions of dark patches they'd already passed. But she didn't argue. She headed for it, and just as she thought they were about to walk into a wall of rock, the darkness deepened and seemed to embrace them.

"We made it," she said, relief making her feel a little giddy.

Quinn reached for the wall of the cave, using it for support as he slid down to land with a grunt. Rebecca kept her gaze on his face, illuminated by a narrow shaft of moonlight. He looked dazed and pale, even in the silvery glow of light. She quickly shed the backpacks and began hunting for the first-aid kit she knew he'd brought. Now that they had stopped, she could see to his injuries.

She flicked on the flashlight and her breath caught in her throat as she got her first good look at him. She swore softly as she surveyed the damage—his shirt was soaked in blood, plastered to his body in several places. Jagged tears split the fabric, providing glimpses of angry red marks on his skin—shallow cuts that had already crusted over with dried blood.

For an endless moment, she couldn't move. She simply stood there, staring at Quinn as memories of Brandon's death assaulted her from all directions. The description of Brandon's injuries ran through her mind, and as she watched, Quinn's features transformed into Brandon's face.

She began to shake, her muscles trembling as anxiety threatened to overtake her. She hadn't been able to help Brandon, hadn't even known he had been attacked until after the fact. She'd sat in front of her computer, blissfully unaware that her fiancé was dying thirty miles away.

Was history about to repeat itself? Was she doomed to lose another man she'd grown to care for, thanks to a violent attack? A wave of helplessness crashed over her, stealing her breath. Quinn was badly hurt, that much was clear. But she didn't know what to do to help him. He wasn't alone like Brandon had been, but given her lack of medical knowledge, he might as well be.

"That bad, huh?" Quinn's voice cut through her rising panic, bringing her back to the moment. He tried to smile, but it was more of a grimace.

Rebecca shook her head, digging deep for a confidence she didn't feel. Even though she was way out of her depth, she wasn't going to let Quinn know. She'd do whatever she could to help him. "I've seen worse." She bit her bottom lip, hoping he hadn't noticed the tremor in her voice.

Rebecca kneeled next to him and gently peeled away his shirt. His chest, shoulders and arms were crisscrossed with wounds, most of them superficial. But there was a deep gash on his side that still oozed blood, and as she leaned around to look at his back, she saw another across his shoulder blades. They looked incredibly painful, but Quinn didn't flinch even as she gently probed the edges of the wounds with her fingertips.

"I think these need stitches," she said, her hands trembling. He wasn't gushing blood, but she knew a slow leak could be just as damaging over time. She fumbled through the first-aid kit, her stomach sinking as she realized there was no suture kit.

"Butterfly strips," Quinn said softly.

"What?"

"You'll have to cut the tape into butterfly strips," he said. "Then you can use them to close my injuries."

The creeping sense of panic receded as Quinn instructed her on how to prepare the tape. Soon, she had a collection of small strips ready to apply to the wounds.

"Let me clean these first," she said. She grabbed a water bottle and poured it over the gash on his side, then dabbed at it with gauze. Working quickly, she pressed the edges of the wound together and applied a line of the makeshift strips to seal it closed. She held her breath as she removed her hand, hoping the tape would stick... If not, she didn't know what else to do.

A few small drops of blood appeared in the spaces between the tape, but the bandages held. Rebecca sighed with relief and smeared a liberal amount of antibiotic ointment on a large square of gauze, which she then taped over the site before moving to the injury on his back. She tried to be gentle, but she could tell from Quinn's shallow breathing he was in a lot of pain.

It took a few minutes to finish patching him up. Quinn didn't speak while she worked, and she didn't know whether to be thankful for the lack of a distraction, or worried that he didn't have the energy to talk. After bandaging the worst of his injuries, she carefully cleaned the shallower cuts and applied antibiotic ointment to each one. It was a little thing that probably wouldn't make a difference, but it helped her to feel like she'd done *something*. Then she retrieved a clean shirt from his pack and draped it around his shoulders.

"You should lie down," she said, pulling a blanket from the pack. They'd left their sleeping bags in the tent at the campsite, but she could make him a crude pallet on the rocky ground. Given the amount of blood he'd lost, it would probably be better for him to stretch out flat rather than stay sitting up.

"You need to call for backup," he said, his voice scratchy. "Do you still have the radio I gave you?"

She reached for her belt, frowning when her hand came up empty. In the chaos of the moment, she'd stuck the radio there before grabbing Quinn to keep him from falling. She hadn't given it a thought since then, taking for granted it would still be there when she was ready to use it. But now she realized it was gone, and she didn't have a clue as to where she'd lost it. Back at the campsite? Or had it fallen off somewhere along the trail, its escape from her waistband unnoticed in the rush to get to safety?

She cursed softly, despair rising in her chest once again. Maybe her phone had service… She clung to the tendril of hope as she dug her cell from her pocket and glanced at the display.

No such luck.

Rebecca sucked in her cheeks as she considered her options. She could leave Quinn and head back out into the night in search of the radio. Or she could stay here and wait for morning. Neither option was appealing. Quinn seemed fine for now, but there was no guarantee he would stay that way for long. What if she left and he needed her? What if his attacker came back to finish the job and found Quinn alone and helpless?

But if she waited until morning, they'd have to go that much longer without help. If she managed to find the radio and call in for assistance, people would set out right away. Sure, they'd have to wait a few hours until anyone arrived, but that was better than waiting all night.

Could she find the radio, though? The waxing moon provided a nice glow, but it was still quite dark. What where the odds she'd be able to find the small monitor, and then find the cave again? She wasn't familiar with these trails or the terrain. And with the way their luck was going right now, she'd probably slip on some gravel and fall off the side of the mountain before she could get back to Quinn.

I'll stay here, she decided. She couldn't risk leaving Quinn alone, not under such precarious circumstances.

"What's wrong?" His voice cut through her thoughts, and for a split second, she debated lying to him so as not to upset him. But she dismissed the idea almost immediately—Quinn deserved to know the truth of their situation. They were in this together, for better or worse.

"I lost the radio," she confessed. "I think it fell off my belt somewhere along the trail."

Quinn didn't respond, and she began to wonder if he'd heard her. Had he fallen asleep?

"Well," he said finally, "that does put a damper on things."

His mild response was so unexpected she couldn't help but laugh. "That's it?"

"What do you mean?" He sounded puzzled.

Rebecca shook her head, even though she was outside the circle of illumination provided by the flashlight. "You're pretty calm, considering I lost our only means of calling for help. Don't you want to yell at me or something?" In truth, she wished he'd display a bit of anger. She felt terrible, and Quinn's understanding strangely enhanced her guilt. If he would just cooperate and argue with her, she'd have a distraction to focus on, to keep her mind off their predicament.

"I don't think yelling at you is going to bring the radio back," Quinn said logically. "And besides, I don't have the energy right now."

"Fair enough." She rummaged in one of the bags and pulled out a bottle of water. "I think you should probably drink this." She unscrewed the cap and passed the bottle to Quinn, who took it and stared at the label for a moment.

"You've lost quite a bit of blood, if your shirt is any indication. I think the water will help you feel better." She didn't really know if that was true, but it sounded good and it made her feel like she was helping him.

Quinn lifted one shoulder and grimaced as the movement caused him pain. "Probably can't hurt," he muttered, taking a healthy swallow.

Rebecca watched him drink, the tension gradually leaving her muscles as she realized he wasn't going to collapse in front of her eyes. Now that they could rest, hopefully Quinn would regain some of his strength before the sun rose again.

She idly played the beam of the flashlight across the walls of the cave, exploring their surroundings. The red rock surface was irregular, dotted with pits and a few small holes here and there. The silk threads of spiderwebs glistened in the light, making her shudder. Best not to think about what creepy-crawlies might be living here...

"How did you know about this place?" Quinn had to be tired, but she wanted to hear his voice. It was selfish, she knew, but she felt very alone and scared. She needed to know he was still there, or her imagination would get the best of her.

"It's my job." His voice was heavy with fatigue and pain, but he took a deep breath and spoke again. "I found it not long after I started working in the park. I figured if I was in the area and ever needed an emergency shelter, this would do."

"You're the ultimate Boy Scout," she said, admiring his foresight. "Always prepared."

"Words to live by."

"Speaking of living, do you think anything calls this place home?" She tried to sound casual, but she couldn't disguise the note of worry in her voice.

"You mean like a mountain lion or a bear?"

Or a snake or a giant spider, she thought. "Well, yeah."

"Probably not," he said. "There are no bears in the park, and I don't smell any evidence of a cat."

"You can smell them?"

"Sometimes. It's a musky scent, maybe mixed with blood from a recent meal, or scat if they've been marking their territory."

"Oh." Rebecca felt even more out of her depth. If Quinn wasn't here, she wouldn't last a hot minute on her own.

"But like I said, there's no mountain lion here."

She let out her breath. "Okay. I believe you."

"Good. Now turn off the flashlight so we can get some rest."

"I don't think I'll be able to sleep tonight," she said.

"Probably not," he replied. "But we need to save the batteries. And we don't want to advertise our position, in case he's looking for us."

Quinn didn't need to define who "he" was—given Harry's earlier absence from the campsite, who else could have attacked Quinn? Rebecca hoped she'd scared Harry away with her gun, but it was possible he'd gone back to his campsite, gathered his friends and some weapons, and set out again to finish the job.

She flicked off the light, her stomach twisting a bit as absolute blackness enveloped them. She'd never been afraid of the dark before, but tonight she felt very small and alone.

"Come here." Quinn's voice was soft but kind, as if he knew what she was feeling.

She scooted closer to him, moving carefully so as not to hurt him. "Do you need something?"

"Yes," he replied. "To hold you."

Her heart warmed at his words. She found his hand in the dark, and he guided her to lie alongside him. He threw his arm over her torso, a warm, heavy weight that anchored her in place. "It's going to be okay," he whispered.

She laughed weakly. "Isn't that supposed to be my line? You're the one who's hurt. I should be comforting you, not the other way around."

"We can help each other," he said. His breath was warm against her skin. Against all odds, Rebecca felt her body relax. The ground was hard and cold, the darkness hid any number of creatures she did not want to think about, Quinn was injured and she'd lost their only means of calling for help, and there was a very real possibility Harry and his friends were even now hunting for them. She should be wound tighter than a coiled spring, but the tension in her muscles eased and her panic slowly drained away. Their situation was definitely not ideal, but she wasn't alone. She had Quinn by her side, and that made all the difference.

"Try to sleep," she said softly. "I'll keep an eye out." She bent her knee, drawing her leg up so her gun was within easy reach. The chances of them being found tonight were small, but if Harry and his cohorts showed up she wasn't going to be caught unawares.

"Wake me in a bit," Quinn said, his voice sleepy. "You need rest, too."

"All right," she lied. She had no intention of disturbing Quinn, but she knew he wouldn't sleep unless she agreed.

He let out a sigh, and after a few minutes, his breathing settled into the deep, regular rhythm of sleep.

Rebecca stared into the darkness, her thoughts racing and her heart filled with emotions she wasn't sure she wanted to name. Seeing Quinn at the mercy of his attacker had taken years off her life. She'd responded without thinking, firing at the masked man before stopping to consider that she might miss and hit Quinn instead. Her shock and fear had driven her actions, and now that the immediate threat had passed, she was angry with herself for letting her emotions rule.

It wasn't the first time she'd let her heart take the lead where Quinn was concerned. Ever since she'd met him, Rebecca had felt drawn to him on a visceral level, one not subject to logic. Her attraction to Quinn and the feelings she'd developed for him were larger than life, something she couldn't control or contain. She simply had to accept them, and learn to deal with the consequences.

As she felt the warmth of his breath on her skin, she realized her attachment to Quinn was no longer casual, or a flight of fancy she could dismiss as the by-product of a stressful situation. No, it went much deeper than that. She'd fallen in love with the man, against her better judgment and despite any number of reasons why she shouldn't. For the first time since losing Brandon, her heart was making itself known. For a long time, she'd feared losing Brandon had meant the end of her ability to love. Now she realized her heart had been broken, but it wasn't dead. It had simply gone into hibernation, coating itself with a protective layer of ice so that it could heal in peace. Now that she was starting to feel again, it was clear she was tougher than she'd known. She'd always carry the scars from Brandon's death, but like an oyster with a grain of sand, her heart had absorbed the blows of his loss and turned them into a pearl of strength.

Quinn sighed in his sleep, his arm tightening around her for an instant before his muscles relaxed again. Even unconscious, he was determined to keep her close. Did that mean he returned her love? She knew he cared for her, but it wasn't clear if his feelings had deepened. Everyone grieved at their own pace, and it was possible Quinn wasn't ready to love again. Possible, too, that he might never be ready. The thought made her stomach twist, but it was a risk she had to acknowledge.

And if he didn't return her love? What then? She couldn't force the man to open his heart. All she could do was confess her feelings and hope for the best.

Her heart fluttered in her chest as she imagined saying those three all-important words. How would

Quinn respond? Would he smile and embrace her, or freeze in shock? Either way, she had to know. If she'd learned anything from her past, it was that life was too short. She couldn't afford to waste time, especially not when something as important as love was involved. She'd take her chances and deal with the fallout, come what may.

But not tonight.

She shifted a bit, trying to dislodge a rock under her hip without waking Quinn. He didn't move, which both pleased and worried her. He'd been through a lot tonight, and she wanted him to rest. But she remained hyperaware of his breathing, scared his injuries were worse than she knew and that he might slip away without her noticing. For the millionth time, she kicked herself for losing the radio. Thanks to her carelessness, Quinn had to spend the night on the cold ground with no chance of rescue. She'd never forgive herself if he suffered any permanent effects from this ordeal.

"Please be okay," she whispered into the darkness. "Don't leave me."

She might not know the extent of Quinn's feelings, but one thing was certain. If she lost him now, her heart would truly break.

Everything hurt.

Quinn let out a soft grunt as he emerged from the fog of sleep into a haze of pain. The cold from the ground had seeped into his bones, leaving them

aching and feeling brittle. His muscles hurt, too—
they were stiff and unyielding, like ropes stretched
to the breaking point. His head throbbed in time with
his heartbeat, and he was desperately thirsty. But he
didn't dare move. He knew on an instinctive level
that the aches and twinges he was dealing with now
were nothing compared to the agony that awaited him
once he really woke up. He could sense the oncom-
ing pain, a malevolent black presence lurking on the
edges of his consciousness. Maybe if he played possum long enough it would grow tired of waiting on
him and move on to the next victim…

"Quinn? Are you awake?"

Rebecca's voice was quiet, as if she was afraid of
disturbing him. Unless he missed his guess, she was
giving him a chance to pretend he hadn't heard her.
But he couldn't ignore her, no matter how bad he felt.
He needed to know she was okay, especially after the
events of last night.

"I'm here," he said. He felt her fingers brush against
his forehead, her touch cool and soothing on his skin.

"How are you?"

Quinn carefully took a deep breath, bracing himself. Then he cracked open his eyelids to focus on
her face.

Rebecca leaned over him, her scent wafting
around him as she leaned closer. Her body blocked
out his view of the sky beyond the cave, but he saw
the glow of pink light around her and realized dawn
was well underway. Time to get moving. Hopefully,

Harry and his friends would be sleeping off the effects of alcohol and he and Rebecca could get out of the area before the young men woke up and thought to start looking for them.

"I survived," he said. Then he realized something. "Did you stay up all night? I told you to wake me so I could help keep an eye out."

Rebecca arched one eyebrow as she stared down at him. "Yeah, like I was really going to do that. You needed the rest."

His irritation fled, replaced by a mixture of guilt and sheepishness. "I'm sorry you stayed up all night. You must be exhausted."

"I'm fine," she said. But the dark circles under her eyes told a different story. It looked like they were both in for a rough day.

"We should get moving." Quinn forced his body to respond to his brain's commands. Slowly, awkwardly, he sat up. Pain blazed through him as his body moved, but he gritted his teeth and ignored it as best he could. They couldn't stay here all day, especially since they had no way of calling for help. Their only choice was to move, so he was simply going to have to deal with the discomfort.

Rebecca helped him lean against the wall of the cave. "Are you sure you're okay?" Her tone was heavy with doubt, and Quinn wondered just how bad he looked. "You're pretty pale."

"I'll be fine," he assured her. "Just need to drink something."

She fished a bottle of water out of the pack and passed it to him. "I think you might be overly optimistic about the restorative powers of water. What about some food?"

The thought of eating made his stomach turn, but he knew she was right. He nodded and accepted an apple and granola bar.

"It's not a gourmet meal, but it's better than nothing," she said.

They ate in silence. The food didn't taste good to Quinn, but he dutifully chewed and swallowed. Rebecca sat across from him, watching him like a hawk.

"If you keep staring at me like that, you're going to give me a complex."

She blinked, realization dawning on her face. "Oh, sorry," she said. She stopped talking, but he could tell by the set of her mouth there was more she wanted to say.

"What is it?" he asked gently.

She shook her head and blinked hard. *She's trying not to cry*, he realized. A wave of tenderness washed over him, and he reached out to touch her knee. "Rebecca?" he said softly.

"It's nothing," she said, swiping her eyes. "I'm just overly tired."

He wanted to pull her into his arms, but the pulsing aches in his side and back warned him against trying it. "Last night was pretty scary," he said, understanding her delayed reaction. She'd done such a great job of holding everything together in the moment—scaring off his attacker, dragging him up the mountain to the cave, tending to his wounds and watching over him all night. Was it any wonder she was feeling the strain of the past few hours?

"That's an understatement," she said drily. "Did you get a good look at the man who attacked you?"

He shook his head. "He wore a bandana just below his eyes. But I think it was Harry."

"So do I," she said grimly. "I should have never let that bastard go—I should have found a way to keep him in custody."

She began to gather up the remnants of their breakfast, clearly looking for a distraction. Quinn let her tidy up, understanding her reaction. He was no stranger to guilt, even when he had no cause to feel bad. But he had something to say to her, and he needed her to hear it, no matter how awkward it might be.

He waited until she was left with nothing to do but brush imaginary crumbs off her shirt. "Rebecca."

She looked up at him, her eyes wide at the seriousness in his voice. "What? Are you okay? Do you need anything?" She leaned forward, one hand reaching for the bag with the medical supplies.

Quinn shook his head. He reached out and touched her cheek. "I need to thank you. For last night. You saved my life."

She waved her hand, trying to brush aside his gratitude. He grabbed it and squeezed gently. "Don't do that. What you did yesterday was amazing. I don't think I could have handled things any better."

Her eyes shone with an emotion he couldn't name. "I'm just glad you're okay now. You really scared me."

"I know, and I'm sorry. I scared myself, too, if it makes you feel any better."

She laughed softly. "It doesn't."

"I mean it, though. The only reason I made it through last night was because of you. There's no one else I'd rather have by my side."

Her cheeks flushed a pretty pink, and she opened her mouth. "Quinn, I—" She stopped, letting her words hang in the air between them.

His heart began to pound. What was she going to say? His mind filled in the blanks with what he hoped to hear, those three little words so packed with emotion. His feelings for Rebecca were growing by the moment, but did she feel the same? He waited in silence, the moment growing heavy with possibility as he waited for her to finish her thought.

She cleared her throat. "I, uh, I hope we can find the radio on the trail back," she said lamely.

Disappointment was a small stone in his stomach. "I hope so, too," he said. *What did you expect?* he chided himself silently. *That she would profess her undying love in the middle of a cave?* He knew it was irrational to feel let down, but his heart wasn't exactly logical. Besides, there was nothing stopping him from making the first move. There was no reason why he couldn't confess his feelings to Rebecca. He couldn't let the fear of rejection rule his life, especially where she was concerned.

I'll tell her, he decided. He opened his mouth, then thought better of it. The cave wasn't exactly an ideal location, and he still felt terrible. He didn't want her to mistake his feelings as overzealous gratitude for her actions last night. Better to wait a bit until their circumstances improved. That way, she would know he truly meant what he said.

"I still can't believe I lost it," she said, oblivious to his inner monologue. He could hear the guilt in her voice and knew she blamed herself for their situation.

"Stop beating yourself up over it," he replied. "It was an accident, plain and simple."

"Yeah," she acknowledged. "But I still feel bad."

"If I had been the one to lose the radio would you be angry?"

She gave him a puzzled look. "No. Of course not."

"Then be just as nice to yourself," he said.

She studied him for a moment, as if trying to gauge his sincerity. A slow smile spread across her face. "I hadn't thought of it that way," she said. "You make a good point."

"It's been known to happen," he said drily.

"Do you want to stay here while I go look for the radio?"

He shook his head before she'd even finished asking the question. "No," he said flatly. No matter how bad he felt, he wasn't about to let her wander off alone. The morning light made last night's danger seem remote, but Harry and his friends were still out there. Quinn wasn't going to be able to relax until they made it back to civilization and the police had locked up the group.

Rebecca frowned. "I don't think it's a good idea for you to try hiking. Not to be overly negative, but you don't look great. If you exert yourself, you might make your injuries even worse."

She was right, but he didn't see any other options. They had to get out of this cave and back to the ranger station. The only way that was going to happen was if they walked.

"I'll be fine," he said, hoping it was the truth. "We'll just take it slow."

Rebecca still looked doubtful, but she didn't say anything.

Quinn took a deep breath and pushed himself up. Pain bloomed in his side and shoulder blades, making him sway a bit on his feet. He clenched his jaw and closed his eyes, searching for balance. After a few seconds, the knife edge of agony dulled and he could think again.

He could do this. He had to do this—he didn't have another choice.

"Quinn?"

He held up a hand, acknowledging her unspoken question.

"I'm okay. Just need to get moving and loosen everything up."

She tugged at the hem of his shirt, lifting the fabric to study his bandages critically.

"I don't see any fresh blood," she said. "Hopefully, they won't reopen as we walk."

"Fingers crossed." Feeling marginally better, he tried for a smile. "Shall we?"

Rebecca shouldered the packs and slipped her arm around his waist. "Might as well."

They began the trek back to the campsite, one careful step at a time. Rebecca let him set the pace, and Quinn focused on putting one foot in front of the other. It was slow going, but after a while his muscles did begin to loosen a bit and the pain dulled.

They were about fifty feet from the camp when Rebecca let out a triumphant yelp. "There it is," she exclaimed. She released her hold on him and darted forward, intent on an object lying a few yards away. She scooped it up and turned back to him, her smile wide and one of relief.

"Now we can get some help," she said, fiddling with the controls on the walkie-talkie. She wasted no time calling the station, and Quinn provided their location.

"We're on the way," said Aaron, one of Quinn's fellow park rangers. "But given your location, it's going to take some time to get to you. Are you in a safe place to wait?"

"We'll stay at the tents," Quinn said. "That will make it easier to find us."

"Excellent," Aaron said. He signed off, and Quinn released a sigh of relief. They weren't totally safe yet, but at least help was coming.

"Are they going to bring a stretcher?" Rebecca

asked. She sounded anxious, and he realized she was still worried about him hiking back.

Quinn shook his head. "Horses, more likely." The animals were adept at navigating the trails, and he would be more than happy to get off his feet.

Rebecca slid her arm around him again and they started toward the tent. The fabric was bright in the sun, a beacon calling him home. Oh, it would be so nice to sit down and rest! He didn't want to admit it to Rebecca, but he was rapidly losing energy. He needed to rest, or he might very well fall over.

After what felt like a small eternity, they reached the tent. Quinn pulled aside the flap, his thoughts consumed with the promise of crawling inside to collapse on his sleeping bag.

But the bag was already occupied.

A tangle of hair caught his eye, and he jerked back before his mind had fully registered the sight of the dead woman in the characteristic pose. His heart dropped to his feet, his stomach cramping as realization dawned.

"Not again." He cursed, anger and fear rising in his chest.

"What's wrong?" Rebecca leaned over to look inside the tent. She stiffened and jerked back almost immediately. "Oh, no," she whispered.

Quinn sank to the ground, the roar of blood filling his ears as adrenaline and shock set his heart racing. "Oh, yes," he said grimly. "The bastard has done it again."

Chapter 13

It was late when Rebecca finally pulled in to the hospital parking lot. After discovering the most recent victim of the Yoga Killer, she'd immediately radioed for the police, and then she and Quinn had passed an uncomfortable few hours while waiting for help to arrive. The park rangers had arrived first, and she'd insisted Quinn leave right away to get medical attention. He hadn't wanted to go, but fortunately Aaron and the other rangers had talked some sense into him. They'd helped him mount one of the horses, and Aaron had stayed with her while Quinn and two others headed back.

The police had arrived soon after, along with a team from the coroner's office. Rebecca had worked the scene with them, snapping photos and cataloging observations in the hopes of catching a break in this case.

It was clear this victim didn't fit the killer's usual pattern. The woman was older than the other victims, and her hair was dark brown, not red. Most telling of all, though, was her apparent cause of death—she'd apparently been stabbed several times, not strangled like the other women.

"Stabbed, just like Harry said," she muttered to herself as she parked under a light. Had he decided to stop masking his identity since she'd already questioned him? Or had he grown so angry after his interrupted attack on Quinn that he'd let his rage take over? Either way, the killer had turned a corner. He was no longer displaying the cold calculation that was characteristic of his earlier murders. Now he was driven by emotion, and she knew from here on out his crimes would be increasingly violent.

She'd told the police about the attack last night, and they had assured her they would arrest Harry and his friends as soon as possible. But that had been several hours ago, and she still hadn't gotten a call from the department telling her they were in custody. What was taking so long? She knew they were a small force, but this case was a priority. It shouldn't take that long to find Harry and his friends—she'd told them the exact location of their campsite.

After turning off the engine, she pulled out her

cell phone and dialed the police chief. He answered on the third ring, sounding harried. "Yes?"

"Chief, it's Rebecca Wade. Have your men been able to arrest Harrison Chambers and his associates?"

The man sighed heavily. "No. Not yet."

Impatience rose in her chest, and she bit her lip to keep from snapping at the man. "Is there anything I can do to help?"

"Not unless you're psychic," he said sarcastically. "We can't find him."

"He wasn't at the campsite?"

"No. We went there soon after your tip, but the men were gone. We're still searching for them."

"I see." She released a sigh of her own, knowing the case had just gotten more complicated. It wasn't a total surprise that Harry and his friends had left the area, especially in the wake of this latest murder. But she was a bit puzzled by the timing—she'd used the binoculars to watch their camp soon after she and Quinn had arrived back at the tent, and she'd seen the men sleeping in their bags out in the open. Given the number of empty beer cans strewn around the site, she'd assumed they would be passed out for most of the day, making them easy pickings for the police.

They must have left while I was busy at the scene. After the rangers and the forensics team had arrived, she'd been occupied with helping to process the site. That must have been when the men had left, which meant she had no idea in which direction they'd gone or at what time they'd escaped.

"I'll let you know when we find them," the chief promised. She heard the fatigue in his voice and knew he must be feeling overwhelmed. A serial killer wasn't the kind of thing a small-town police department was equipped to handle, and as the body count mounted, so did the pressure to make an arrest.

"Thanks." She signed off and tossed the phone back into her purse. Then she ran a hand over her face, trying to erase the strain and fatigue of the day. She didn't want to walk into Quinn's room feeling so beat down.

She'd hated being apart from him today, but knowing he'd been getting medical attention had eased her mind. Last night had been one of the hardest of her life. She'd sat vigil over Quinn, watching him like a hawk, her ears tuned for any change in his breathing, any hitch or noise that would indicate he was in distress. She'd been so afraid of falling asleep, convinced that if she let down her guard, he'd slip away and she'd wake to find him dead. It was silly, but she'd managed to convince herself that if she stayed awake and kept watch over him, he wouldn't be able to die.

The night had seemed endless, an infinite loop of time repeating over and over in her own personal version of hell. At least Harry and his friends hadn't found them—she probably could have taken on Harry by herself, especially with her gun—but if his friends had shown up as well, she'd have been in trouble. A small, irrational part of her was a little disappointed she hadn't had another go at Harry. Her anger at him had built over time, and she wasn't too noble to admit she wanted revenge for his having hurt Quinn. It would feel so good to be the one to bring him down, but she knew it was better to let the justice system do the work for her. It might take more time, but in the long run, she'd have more satisfaction knowing he was rotting in a jail cell.

She stepped into the hospital, glancing at the directory posted on the wall. The characteristic smell invaded her nose as she headed for the elevator, and she shook her head. How was it that all these places smelled the same?

It didn't take long to find Quinn's room—the hospital was small, and didn't have that many beds. She hesitated at the door, wondering if he was asleep. Maybe she should come back in the morning, let him get his rest. But the need to see him was almost overpowering, and she knew she couldn't wait that long.

I'll just poke my head in the room, she told herself. If he was asleep, she wouldn't wake him. But she needed to catch a glimpse of him, to know for sure that he was okay and would recover.

Moving carefully, she pushed open the door a crack and winced as the hinges gave out a high squeak. The room was quiet, the low thrum of the IV pump the only sound she could hear.

Quinn was lying still in the bed, his eyes closed and his body relaxed. Rebecca rested her eyes on him, her heart warming as she watched him breathe. The last of the evening light cast the room in a soft glow, giving his skin a golden hue. She saw the edges of several white bandages peeking out from under his hospital gown and shuddered as she recalled the extent of his injuries. But the tension inside her eased as she realized he was truly okay. His features were relaxed, his face no longer tight with the pain and discomfort that had plagued him even as he'd slept last night.

Satisfied for the moment, Rebecca began to ease back out of the room. But as she started to move, Quinn stirred. He shook his head slowly, then opened his eyes and fixed them on her. He blinked, then his face broke out in a smile that was so beautiful it nearly broke her heart.

"Hey," he said. His voice was raspy, but it was the loveliest sound she'd ever heard. He lifted one hand off the bed, reaching for her. "I was hoping you'd come by."

She stepped into his room, letting the door snick closed behind her. She headed for the chair in the corner, intending to pull it over to the bed. But Quinn patted the mattress and angled his legs to the side, making room for her. Unable to pass up this offer, she sat carefully, trying not to jostle him.

"I'm sorry it took so long," she said. "I know it's a cliché, but I came as soon as I could."

"I know," he said simply. "I figured you'd be busy, given our discovery this morning." A shadow crossed his face and her own mood dipped as well.

"I can't believe he did it again," Quinn continued.

"I guess I assumed he wouldn't have the time to hurt anyone else after attacking me last night."

Rebecca nodded. "I don't think he'd planned this one," she said. "You could tell by the scene he wasn't as composed or calm. This was a crime of opportunity and anger. He was probably frustrated because he hadn't managed to kill you, so he found this woman and took his rage out on her."

Quinn shook his head. "That poor lady."

"I think it really was a case of being in the wrong place at the wrong time. She doesn't fit his victim pattern—her hair is brown, not red. And she's older than the others. Given the timing of her murder, she was likely someone camping in the park and he snatched her when she was asleep or when she moved off to use the bathroom."

"Have there been any reports of a missing camper? Surely she wasn't alone."

Rebecca lifted one shoulder. "I'm not sure. The police are investigating that angle, but I haven't heard yet if anyone has noticed she's gone."

Quinn was quiet a moment. "When I saw her this morning..." He trailed off, then cleared his throat. "I think I saw blood in the tent."

"You did," Rebecca confirmed. "That's another change to his pattern. He didn't strangle this woman. He stabbed her."

Quinn swallowed hard, his Adam's apple bobbing in the column of his throat. "I see." He looked upset, and Rebecca noticed the green line on the monitor pick up speed as his heart began to pound.

"None of this was your fault," she said. "Tell me you understand that."

"I suppose," he said, staring at the blanket covering his legs. "That's what the police said when they came by to talk to me today. But if I'd known he was going to kill another woman, I could have tried harder to overpower him."

"He had a knife," she pointed out. "You had, what? A spade? It wasn't exactly a fair fight."

Quinn brushed aside her logic. "I know. But I still feel bad."

She took his hand, giving it a soft squeeze. "I understand." *That's what I love about you.* The words were on the tip of her tongue, but she clamped her lips shut. Now was not the time for declarations of the heart.

"What did the doctors say about your injuries?"

He shrugged slightly. "That I'm lucky. None of the wounds were too deep, at least from their perspective."

Rebecca noticed an empty bag hanging from his IV pole. "You needed blood?"

"Yeah. Just a little bit to top me off. They stitched me up and told me I'll have some good scars."

"Oh, well." She tried for a laugh. "I guess it could have been worse."

"Most definitely." The corner of his mouth tipped up in a smile. "The doctor stitching me up was impressed with your handiwork. Said he couldn't have done a better job himself."

"Yeah, right." She felt her cheeks flush at the overblown compliment. "I'm sure that's not true."

"I don't know about that," Quinn remarked. "I think he was a new intern. He looked all of twelve years old."

Rebecca just shook her head, smiling despite herself.

Quinn's eyes tracked over her face, his gaze soft and full of affection. "Did you get any sleep last night?"

She considered bluffing, but realized there was no point. She'd caught a glimpse of herself in the bathroom mirror about an hour ago and knew her face was lined with fatigue and stress. "Not really."

"There's plenty of room in this bed," he offered.

Rebecca lifted an eyebrow at his offer. "No offense, but I think your eyesight might have been affected by the attack. That's a pretty narrow mattress."

"I'll scoot over."

She was sorely tempted to let him. Exhaustion pulled at her limbs, making her body feel heavy and sluggish. The thought of driving back to her hotel was enough to make her want to cry.

"Please?" Quinn said. "I'll sleep better if I'm next to you."

Her heart flip-flopped in her chest and she was lost. "Okay," she said, nodding her acceptance. "But only because I want you to get your rest."

Quinn's smile lit up the room. He moved carefully, scooting over to one side of the mattress. He lifted the sheet and wriggled his eyebrows in invitation. "It's not the Ritz, but at least the place is clean."

Rebecca toed off her shoes and slid into the bed beside him. Her hair and skin felt gritty with desert sand, but she was too tired to care. Quinn fit his body around hers, his chest against her back, his warmth seeping into her bones. She relaxed with a sigh, reveling in the simple pleasure of stretching out on a mattress after a sleepless night and long day.

"Perfect." Quinn's sigh was soft in her ear. "Just what I needed."

Me, too, she thought. She opened her mouth to respond, but sleep beckoned her like a long-lost friend. She closed her eyes and surrendered to its pull with a sigh.

He strode down the hall of the hospital, feeling more confident by the moment. At this time of day the halls were mostly empty—visiting hours were long over, so only staff members were around to see him. No one gave him a second look as he walked, and why should they? With his blue scrubs and white coat, he looked like he belonged there.

He moved with confidence, nodding as he passed various nurses and doctors. He'd learned long ago the best way to blend in was to act naturally, and he was a pro. The fact that people were seeing his face didn't bother him; nothing about his appearance stood out, and his behavior was unremarkable. Tomorrow, when the police were here interviewing potential witnesses, no one would think to talk about him. He was like the wallpaper—present, but forgotten as soon as you looked away.

It didn't take long to find Gallagher's room. The place wasn't that big to begin with, and he was one of only three patients on the floor. But rather than head straight for his target, he stopped at the nurses' station at the far end of the hall.

"Hello." He smiled pleasantly as he slid the box he carried onto the counter. "We had a patient's family drop these off about an hour ago, and figured we might share the wealth."

The woman behind the desk eyed his offering with curiosity. "What is it?" She stood and reached for the lid.

"Doughnuts," he said. "Said they got them at the grocery store. They're actually pretty good if you warm them up a bit first."

"Thanks a lot," she said, smiling at him. "It's almost time for my break, and this will be a nice treat."

"Want me to put them in your break room?" he offered.

She shook her head. "I'll do it." She glanced at the monitors behind the desk, then reached for the box. "Be right back."

"Take your time," he said. "I can hold down the fort."

He waited until she was halfway down the hall

before making his move. He headed for Gallagher's room and slipped inside, his hand going to his waistband and the knife he had sheathed there. Quinn had gotten away the first time. He wasn't going to be so lucky now.

He approached the bed and drew up short at the sight that greeted him. Gallagher wasn't alone—there was a woman lying next to him. He squinted in the dim light, trying to make out her face.

It's the FBI agent, he realized with a small shock. The woman who had interrupted him last night.

He hadn't planned on attacking Quinn last night. He'd been out walking the trail, scouting for a good spot to leave his next victim. But when he'd seen Gallagher alone on the path, he hadn't been able to pass up the opportunity to hurt him. He wanted Quinn to feel pain, to suffer as he'd been doing for the past few years. He'd acted on instinct, lashing out, even though killing Quinn would mean the end of his fun.

Anger filled him at the memory of the woman's interference. Gallagher had been on the ropes—they'd both known it. A few more strikes, and Quinn would have been bleeding to death in the dirt, like he deserved. But she'd ruined everything.

He tightened his grip on the handle of his knife, anticipation thrumming through his veins. He hadn't foreseen this development, but he wasn't disappointed. The prospect of killing Quinn had kept him motivated all day, making him smile whenever he imagined it. The fact that he was also going to take care of that meddling bitch was just the icing on the cake.

He slipped the knife free of its sheath as he studied the sleeping pair. They looked so peaceful, completely oblivious to their fate. Which one should he dispatch first? Quinn, or the woman? Either way, he had to be quick about it. He couldn't have them waking up and sounding the alarm while he worked.

The woman, he decided. She was closest to him, the easiest target. He'd cut her throat and then do the same to Quinn, leaving them to bleed out in each other's arms.

How romantic. And exactly what Quinn deserved, after taking his woman away from him.

He reached for her, but just before he made contact with her hair, inspiration struck. He could kill both of them now, that much was true. But it would be so much more satisfying to make the moment last. If he acted now, it would all be over too quickly. He wouldn't be able to savor the justice of it all, to see the anguish in Quinn's eyes as he watched the woman he loved die while he sat there helpless.

He smiled as a new plan took shape in his mind. He'd have to be patient, but he'd waited this long. What was a few more days, especially when the payoff would be so sweet?

He returned the knife to its sheath and took a step back. Quinn stirred, briefly opening his eyes. He made a small sound, but the room was dark and the man knew Gallagher didn't recognize him.

"Just checking on you," the man said easily. "Is this your wife?"

"Not yet," Quinn mumbled. His arm tightened around the woman as he fell back to sleep.

A swell of satisfaction rose in his chest. Oh, yes. Much better to wait to kill them.

He backed out of the room, being careful to move quietly so as not to disturb them. Now that he had the makings of a new plan, he didn't want to risk detection. He gave the couple one last look at the door.

"Enjoy your time together," he whispered. "It won't last long."

Chapter 14

Rebecca woke suddenly, transitioning from sleep to consciousness so quickly it was disorienting.

She sat up, blinking as she took in her surroundings. Hospital room. Her shoes on the floor.

Quinn.

She turned to find him sleeping peacefully next to her, his big body stretched out on the thin mattress. He had to be uncomfortable, lying near the edge of the bed like that, but he didn't stir. A rush of love nearly stole her breath as she realized he'd held her all night. Even in sleep, even while injured, he took care of her.

How did I get so lucky?

She eased herself off the bed, trying not to jostle him. She could use a lot more sleep, but she heard voices in the hall and knew the nurses and doctors would be making their rounds soon. She wasn't ashamed to have slept next to Quinn all night, but she didn't want anyone else to know about it. That was a private, special time between them, something she would always cherish. She didn't want to share it with the staff.

Her phone buzzed just as she settled into the recliner in the corner. A glance at the display told her it was the police chief calling.

"Yes?" She spoke quietly as she pushed herself up and headed for the door. Quinn needed to sleep as long as possible—she didn't want to be the one to wake him up.

"We found Harry."

Rebecca slipped into the hall and leaned against the wall. Something in the man's tone told her this wasn't a good development.

"You don't sound happy about it," she said.

"He's dead."

Rebecca swore a blue streak. The police chief sighed softly. "That was my reaction, too," he said.

"Where, when and how?" she asked. She knew she was being rude, but she was too frustrated to care about manners right now.

"His parents found him this morning. The *how* and *when* are a bit tougher to answer. His mother said she heard him come in late last night, but didn't know the time."

"Any signs of foul play?"

"No. Looks like he came home drunk, passed out

and asphyxiated on his own vomit. Still, we'll have to wait for the coroner's report for the final pronouncement, but there are no obvious signs of injury aside from some scratches on his arms."

Rebecca's thoughts swirled as she considered the chief's words. Quinn had said he'd gotten a few swipes in with his spade, which would explain the scratches on Harry's arms. But what had killed him? Had he been overcome by guilt after murdering yet another woman and decided to take his own life?

Probably not. In her interview with Harry, she hadn't detected any signs of empathy or consideration for the victims. It was unlikely he'd suddenly grown a conscience.

"I do have some good news, though," the chief offered.

"I'll take it," Rebecca said. Maybe they'd found the murder weapon by his body, or some other evidence tying him to the crimes...

"We know who the latest victim is," the man said. "Her name is Olivia Parsons. She and some friends had set up camp in the park, a couple miles away from where you found her body. According to her friends, she'd gotten up to use the bathroom in the middle of the night. They realized this morning she hadn't returned, and alerted the park rangers as soon as they could."

"Have you notified her family yet?"

"That's my next call," the chief said. She heard the note of reluctance in his voice and knew he wasn't looking forward to that conversation. It was never easy to be the bearer of such difficult news, and she didn't envy him his job.

"I'm glad we know her name," Rebecca said, picturing the woman's body as she'd last seen it. Olivia hadn't deserved to die, especially not in such a violent way. The waste of it all fueled Rebecca's anger, but that was a useless emotion. With Harry gone, there was nothing she could do to bring the man to justice. She hoped the families of the victims would take comfort in the fact the killer was dead, but Rebecca wanted more. She wanted him to experience a lifetime of punishment, to spend every moment aware of his loss of freedom, to know he would never again enjoy the simple pleasures in life.

But it was not to be.

"Good work, chief," Rebecca said. "You and your department have done an outstanding job on this investigation."

"Thank you." There was a note of surprise in his voice, as if he hadn't expected the compliment. "My team has been working round-the-clock."

"I appreciate the assistance."

"I would say it's been our pleasure, but that's not exactly the case."

Rebecca smiled, understanding him perfectly. "I know what you mean. I'll try to stop by your office today to wrap up any loose ends."

"See you then."

She ended the call and slipped the phone back into her pocket. For the first time in days, she felt at a loss for what to do next. With the death of her prime suspect, it seemed like her investigation had come to a sudden and unexpected end. Where did that leave her now?

And what did that mean for her and Quinn? She still had a bit of work to do to definitively link Harry to the initial murder victims. But once that was done, she'd no longer have a reason for staying in town. She'd known she and Quinn would eventually have to have The Talk—where their relationship was going, whether they would try to stay together after she went back to Virginia, that kind of thing. But she hadn't thought the issue would come to a head so soon. She'd wanted to go into the discussion with her mind made up about what she wanted for their next steps. Instead, she was still processing her feelings, trying to figure out the best plan. She felt like a student who'd been caught without her homework, and she wasn't happy about it.

A woman in a white coat approached Quinn's room. "Are you family of the patient?"

"I'm not related to him," Rebecca replied. "But we're close." That seemed like the best way to summarize their relationship at the moment. She hoped the doctor would speak to her about Quinn's condition, even though she had no blood or legal connection to him.

"What's your name?" the woman asked.

"Rebecca Wade."

The doctor nodded, as if she'd suspected this. "I'm Dr. Allen. I was the attending on call when Mr. Gallagher came in yesterday. He mentioned your name, said we could speak to you regarding his condition."

Rebecca nodded, appreciating his foresight. It seems she needn't have worried—once again, Quinn had thought of everything. "Is he going to be okay?"

Dr. Allen nodded. "Yes. But he's quite lucky. The stab injuries were mostly superficial, and the ones that are deep didn't penetrate his abdominal wall. He lost quite a bit of blood thanks to the number of cuts, but he should make a full recovery."

Rebecca's mood lightened as the weight of worry dissolved away. Quinn had told her as much yesterday, but it was good to hear the doctor confirm his words. "I'm so happy to hear that."

The woman smiled. "He's going to need to take things easy for the foreseeable future. He doesn't strike me as the type to willingly rest, so you'll probably have to be the bad guy and insist upon it."

"I can do that," Rebecca assured her. Quinn wouldn't be happy about the forced break, but she'd do her best to keep him from overdoing it.

"Good," replied the doctor. "I'm going to check his stitches, and if everything looks good, I'll clear him for release today."

"Okay. I think I'll stay out here while you do that." Rebecca had no desire to see Quinn's injuries again, especially not under the bright lights of the hospital room. She'd seen quite enough of his blood already, and didn't need another reminder of the pain he'd endured.

Dr. Allen's eyes took on a knowing gleam. "I won't be long." She disappeared into the room, leaving Rebecca in the hall, alone with her thoughts once more.

"This is unnecessary," Quinn grumbled. "I'm perfectly capable of walking on my own."

Rebecca ignored his protest and slipped her arm around his torso, supporting some of his weight as they started up the stairs to his apartment.

He tried again. "I know the doctor said I had to relax, but don't you think this is taking things a bit far?"

"Nope," she replied. "The last thing I need is for you to fall down the stairs and reopen your wounds or break your leg."

She had a good point, but he was too proud to acknowledge it. Truth be told, he did feel a bit shaky on his feet but he'd never admit that. He didn't want Rebecca to feel like she had to take care of him. She'd done enough of that already, and he knew she was exhausted. If he pretended all was normal, he might be able to convince her to return to her hotel and get some rest. At the very least, maybe she'd agree to take a nap in his bed. It would be nice to have his sheets smell like her again…

They made it down the hall and stopped in front of his door. Had it really been only two days since he'd been here? It seemed like an eternity had passed since he'd packed their bags for Rebecca's reconnaissance mission. Now he was back, bruised and battered and feeling thoroughly wrung out. Maybe next time he should trust his instincts...

He unlocked the door and headed for the couch, collapsing onto the cushions with a sigh. Rebecca closed the door behind him and came to stand by his feet. "Can I get you anything?"

"A beer?" he asked hopefully. He wasn't a big drinker, but it seemed like a good way to celebrate surviving an attack by a knife-wielding serial killer.

Rebecca shook her head. "I don't think alcohol will mix well with the pain pills your doctor sent home with you."

"Likely not." He shrugged and leaned back, propping his feet on the coffee table.

"How about some water instead?"

"I'm fine," he said, waving away her offer. "You don't need to wait on me."

"I don't mind," she said. "It's the least I can do, seeing as how I feel responsible for this whole situation."

Quinn looked up at her, one eyebrow lifted. "Were you the one who stabbed me the other night?"

"No." She lifted a hand to stave off his reply. "But if I hadn't insisted on spying on Harry and his friends, you wouldn't have been attacked."

"It wasn't fun," he admitted. "But maybe it all worked out for the best. Now that Harry is dead..." He trailed off, thinking of all the women the man had killed. "Well, at the very least, the women in the area should be a lot safer now." Rebecca had told him about Harry's death in the car, but it still wasn't clear how the young man had died. Maybe it was wrong of him, but Quinn couldn't bring himself to care about the killer. Death from overdose, alcohol poisoning, accident—it didn't matter, so long as he was gone and his rampage was over.

He still had a hard time thinking of Harry as the murderer. Not because the young man had been such a paragon of virtue. But from what Quinn had seen, Harry wasn't much of a hiker. He'd certainly had the strength to overpower a woman, but would he have really wanted to hike with them first?

"Speaking of Harry," Rebecca said, interrupting his thoughts. She let out a small sigh, a shadow crossing her face. "I need to stop by the police station and talk to the chief. There are a few things I need to discuss with him to close out the case."

"No problem." A pang of disappointment speared his chest at her mention of closing the case, and he immediately felt guilty. He should be happy the murderer was gone and there would be no more victims, but a selfish part of him understood that Rebecca would be leaving soon. He wasn't ready to say goodbye to her, not when there was so much left unsaid between them.

And whose fault is that? he chided himself. If Rebecca didn't know how he felt about her, it was because he hadn't made it clear. He needed to stop waiting for the perfect moment to talk to her— there was never going to be an ideal time. He simply needed to open up the conversation and tell her what was in his heart. Quinn was fairly certain she cared for him as well, but he didn't know what she thought their future should look like. Hell, he wasn't sure if *he* knew what their future should look like. One thing was certain, though—they needed to decide together, and the sooner, the better.

"I'll be back as soon as I can." Concern gleamed in her eyes, and he knew she was worried about leaving him alone.

"Take as long as you need. I'll be fine."

"Can I get you anything before I go? Something to eat or drink?"

He shook his head. "I'm not hungry. But I'll take a kiss."

She smiled and leaned down. She smelled like soap, from the shower she'd taken earlier at the hospital. "I can definitely do that."

Her lips brushed against his, a soft caress that gave him goose bumps. She tasted like coffee, with a hint of the doughnuts they'd shared on the way home from the hospital. He reached for her, wanting to bring her closer so he could deepen the kiss. Holding her all night had been nice, but now he wanted more. A sharp pain lanced his side as his movement pulled the stitches holding his wound closed. He sucked in a breath at the unexpected sensation, his arousal vanishing as his injuries vied for attention.

Rebecca pulled back, her eyes roaming his face. "Hurts?" she asked.

He nodded. "A little. I'd almost forgotten about all the stitches."

"That's not good."

Quinn disagreed. For a moment, it had been wonderful. Kissing Rebecca had made the world disappear. Warmth had spread through him, chasing away his aches and pains. His mind had calmed, his thoughts no longer circling around the killer and his victims. The stress of recent events had eased, and his worries over their future had quieted in the face of their connection. Rebecca was his refuge from the world, and he needed her, now more than ever.

"Are you going to be okay on your own?" There was a note of worry in her voice, and he knew if he expressed any doubt she wouldn't hesitate to stay with him. A selfish part of him considered lying—it would be nice to spend time with her now that they were both safe. But he couldn't abuse her goodwill that way. Trust was an important part of their relationship, and he didn't want to take hers for granted.

"I'll be okay. I'll watch TV and nap until you get back."

"Promise?" She hesitated, clearly torn about leaving him. Quinn knew he was going to have to be a bit more convincing to get her out the door. She might want to stay, but he knew how important it was for her to talk to the police chief. Her dedication and sense of responsibility were two of the qualities he loved most about her, and he didn't want her to feel guilty about leaving him.

He nodded. "I won't do anything more strenuous than walk to the bathroom."

"Okay," she said. "I'm taking your keys so I can lock up behind myself. That way, if you're asleep when I get back I won't have to disturb you."

Quinn smiled, touched by her concern. "That's very thoughtful of you."

"I'll bring food when I come back. If there's anything that sounds especially good to you right now, text me."

"I will." He could tell she was stalling, looking for any excuse to stay. So he shooed her off. "Get going. The chief is waiting for you."

Rebecca hesitated, then bent and pressed a quick kiss to his cheek. "Call me if you need anything," she said. Her blue eyes were warm with affection.

"Maybe we can talk when you get back?" She blinked in surprise at his sudden change of topic, and Quinn wanted to bite his tongue. This was hardly the moment to start such a sensitive conversation! But he felt better after bringing it up—now he had a deadline of sorts, and could no longer find an excuse to postpone telling her about his feelings.

"It's nothing bad," he added, seeing the worry on her face. "I just have some things I'd like to say to you."

Understanding dawned in her eyes and she nodded. "I'd like that," she said, sounding almost shy. "There are things I want to say to you as well."

Quinn's heart skipped a beat as anticipation fizzed in his system. Maybe he didn't need to worry about talking to her after all—if they were both on the same page regarding their feelings for each other, surely they would be able to make everything else work.

She gave him one last smile, then turned and walked out the door, taking his heart with her.

Chapter 15

"Thanks for seeing me on such short notice."

Chief Givens nodded absently and ushered Rebecca into his office. "No problem," he said. "Truth be told, we're looking forward to wrapping up this investigation." He sat behind his desk and gestured for her to take the chair opposite. His expression was a bit apologetic as he glanced at his computer. "We're not really cut out for these kinds of cases," he said, lowering his voice a bit. "Usually, our biggest worry is speeding tickets, maybe a little drunk-and-disorderly. That kind of thing. Murder is a whole different ball game." He shook his head and met her gaze while his computer hummed busily. "I can count on one hand the number of these cases I've encountered in my whole career. At least, I used to be able to…" He trailed off, sounding dismayed.

"I understand," Rebecca said. "Murder investigations are always difficult, and a serial killer is especially disturbing."

"I just can't believe one of our own did this."

Rebecca nodded understandingly. "It's always hard to imagine the people we know are capable of such evil acts."

The man continued as if she hadn't spoken. "I mean, Harry's always been a bit of a wild card. But never in a million years would I have expected him to be guilty of something like this."

"What makes you say that?" Rebecca was curious to hear his thoughts. She'd formed her own impression of Harry based on her earlier interview, but maybe the police chief could give her some insight into Harry's life that would help her find the connections between him and the first victims.

The man shrugged, narrowing his eyes a bit as he considered her question. "He got into trouble on a fairly regular basis, but it was always for low-level stuff. Public intoxication, speeding, even a DUI once. You could tell he was a kid who was frustrated about how his life was going, but he didn't know what to do about it."

Rebecca nodded, agreeing with him. So far, no smoking gun…

"Did his behavior ever escalate? Did he ever show flashes of temper or rage that were uncharacteristic?"

"No. Harry didn't have enough self-control to hide his emotions. You always knew exactly what kind of mood he was in and what he was thinking." The man paused, tilting his head to the side. "I guess that's why I'm still in disbelief. I didn't think he was smart enough to live a double life."

"Maybe he was a better actor than you knew," Rebecca suggested.

"Maybe," Chief Givens replied, sounding a bit doubtful. "Anyway, here are the photos we took at the scene of Harry's death." He swiveled the computer monitor around so she could view the screen. "As you can see, there's nothing to suggest murder." He scrolled quickly through the images, as if this was simply a formality.

"Wait, please," she said. She frowned and reached for the mouse. The chief surrendered it and leaned back with a "have at it" wave of his hand.

Rebecca scrolled through the files again, this time at a slower pace. Sure enough, the chief's description of the scene matched the images. The photos showed Harry, flat on his back in bed, his eyes open and sightless. Dried vomit decorated his chin and the sheets under his head, indicating the most likely cause of death. She turned her attention to his forearms, visible in several of the pictures. Scratches marred his skin, but the red lines appeared close together and ran in parallel tracks. She frowned, zooming in on one of the images. These injuries didn't look like the kind of thing inflicted by a spade. Unless she missed her guess, these wounds resembled those from a cat or a small dog.

Maybe Quinn had been mistaken—perhaps he'd slashed Harry's chest, not his arms? But Harry was shirtless and she saw no marks on his upper arms, his chest or his stomach.

She made a mental note to talk to the medical examiner. It was possible she was mistaken, that the pictures weren't clear enough and she wasn't seeing how bad the scratches truly were. Quinn was certain he'd slashed his attacker, and she believed him. She simply had to recalibrate her expectations. After seeing the severity of Quinn's injuries she'd imagined Harry would sport similar wounds. *But he attacked Quinn with a knife, while Quinn only had a spade*, she reminded herself. It made sense that Harry's scratches would be superficial at best.

Feeling a little better, she perused the rest of the pictures. Harry's room was a mess, with empty beer cans and cigarette packs strewn about the floor. Several bongs decorated his bedside table, the discolored glass a testament to their frequency of use. A ticket stub peeked out from under a bag of weed, and a twenty-dollar bill—

Wait a minute. She scrolled back to the image of the ticket stub. It was a bus ticket, dated the twenty-fifth.

The date of the first murder.

Rebecca's breath caught as she strained to make out the details printed on the paper. It was a ticket from Austin to Alpine. But had Harry really taken the trip? Or was this simply a ruse to give himself an alibi in the event the police ever questioned him about the first murder?

She jotted down the bus company's name—perhaps they had cameras on their buses, and she could obtain the footage from that trip. She scrolled through the remainder of the images, but her thoughts were elsewhere.

If Harry really had been in Austin in the days leading up to the first murder, how had he scouted his victim? And if he'd been on a bus the day Quinn had discovered the body, then Harry wasn't the killer. The medical examiner had already determined the death of the first victim had occurred a few hours before she'd been discovered. That ruled out the possibility Harry had killed her and dumped the body before his trip.

A cold sweat broke out on Rebecca's skin as her thoughts whirled. This changed everything. If Harry really had taken that trip, he wasn't the Yoga Killer. All of the victims had been murdered by the same person, so if he hadn't killed the first woman, he hadn't killed the others, either.

"Do you have the contact information for Harry's parents?"

"Uh, sure," the chief replied. He shuffled through some papers on his desk, then passed her a form. "Here you go. What's up?"

Rebecca ignored the question and quickly dialed

the phone number on the page. She knew it was a little insensitive to call rather than talk to them in person, but she didn't have time to make the drive.

A man answered the phone. Rebecca tried to be as delicate as possible, understanding Harry's father was still trying to process the death of his son. Still, she had to know...

"Mr. Chambers, I realize this is an odd question, but did Harry take any trips recently?"

"I—I don't know," the man said. He sounded exhausted, and she felt a pang of sympathy for him. Even though Harry had been trouble, his parents had still loved him.

"Please," Rebecca persisted. "I wouldn't ask if it wasn't important."

Harry's father sighed. "I think he went to Austin a couple of weeks ago. Had some friends to see out there."

"Do you remember their names?"

"No," he said flatly. "Now if you'll excuse me, I need to get back to my wife."

He hung up the phone before she could say another word. Rebecca glanced at the police chief, who was watching her with a puzzled look on his face.

"Harry may have been in Austin during the first murder," she said shortly.

Understanding dawned on the man's face. "But that means—"

"I know," she said. She reached for the keyboard

and pulled up the internet. "His father said he'd gone to see some friends, but he didn't know their names."

"It's possible he didn't leave town at all," the chief said hopefully. "Maybe he just told his parents he left, but he stayed in the park with the first victim."

"Let's hope," she said, pulling up Harry's Facebook page. She scrolled down, holding out hope that she wouldn't find anything…

"Damn," she said softly.

"What is it?"

She flipped the monitor back toward the chief. "Pictures of Harry and his friends in Austin, time-stamped on the date of the murder."

The man stared at the screen, pressing his lips together. "Maybe the pictures are fake?" he suggested weakly. "People can do a lot of things with Photoshop these days…"

Rebecca shook her head. "I don't think so." Her stomach dropped as the implications of her discovery sank in.

Harry wasn't the killer.

So who was?

She'd been so focused on Harry and his friends, thinking she'd found the murderer. Now that she knew better, she was left with no leads, no other possibilities to explore. Back to square one, with no clues to indicate where she should go next.

How much time had she wasted, trying to catch Harry in a lie? Had she overlooked evidence that would point her in the direction of the real killer?

God, if she hadn't been so single-minded, she wouldn't have insisted on spying on Harry and his friends!

Quinn's face flashed in her mind, a memory of how he'd looked when she had discovered him. Images from that horrible night taunted her as she recalled his blood-soaked shirt and the slippery feel of his skin as she pinched the edges of his wounds together to tape them closed. It was her fault Quinn had been attacked, her fault he'd almost died.

She ran a shaking hand over her face as her guilt blossomed. If not for her mistake, the Yoga Killer would never have encountered Quinn alone on the trail. He wouldn't have tried to murder Quinn, wouldn't have grown so angry when he hadn't been able to finish the job. If not for Rebecca's actions, the man would never have snatched an innocent woman from her campground and killed her in a fit of rage. Her mistake went far beyond trying to pin these crimes on an innocent man—thanks to her, a woman was dead and the man she loved was dealing with the fallout from a brutal attack.

Bile burned the back of her throat. She swallowed hard, feeling sick to her stomach. Doubt landed on her with the force of a hammer blow. Maybe she wasn't cut out for this job anymore. Everyone made mistakes, but this one was different. This error had cost a life and drastically affected another. It wasn't the kind of thing she could simply shrug off or ignore. Her actions had real-world consequences, and because of her misjudgment, this psycho was still out there, free to act again.

And she had no idea where or when he'd strike next.

The doorbell rang just as he pulled cookies out of the oven. Quinn had told Rebecca he'd rest while she was gone, but in truth, he'd been too keyed up to sit quietly and wait for her to return. The anticipation of telling her how he really felt about her filled him with nervous energy, and he'd had to find something to keep his hands and mind occupied. He wasn't much of a baker, but the package of premade dough in his fridge had looked straightforward enough, and the instructions were simple. He glanced at the cookies as he set the tray on the stove top—they seemed fine, and they smelled good. Hopefully, they were edible...

He walked to the door, wondering who was wanting to visit him in the middle of the afternoon. A neighbor, perhaps? Maybe a coworker who had heard he'd been released from the hospital? Or maybe Rebecca had lost his keys, or simply forgotten she had them.

He opened the door and blinked, staring at his visitor in blank surprise before registering his presence. "Justin," he said, his mind scrambling. "It's good to see you again."

Naomi's widower smiled. "How's it going?"

"Uh, I'm okay." Quinn struggled to come up with a reason for this visit. Running in to Justin at the bar a few nights ago had been unusual, and even though they had made vague promises about meeting up for a meal while Justin was in town, Quinn hadn't actually expected to see him again. They had never been close, despite their wives' friendship. "What brings you to my place?"

"I'm headed out in the morning, thought I'd stop by for a drink and say goodbye. Can I come in?"

Quinn wasn't in the mood to chat, but he didn't want to be rude. "This isn't the greatest time," he hedged. "I actually just got out of the hospital this morning."

"Oh, man." Concern flitted across Justin's face as his eyes searched Quinn for obvious signs of injury. "You do look kind of pale. What happened?"

Quinn shrugged, dismissing the question. No way was he going to talk about the attack with Justin. Even though the man had been Naomi's husband, Quinn had never been all that fond of him. He seemed like a nice enough guy, but there was just something about him that rubbed Quinn the wrong way. He always seemed to think he was the smartest guy in the room, a quality Quinn found irritating. And now that Ashley was gone, he didn't have to pretend to like Justin anymore. "I had an accident on the job," he said.

"Nothing too serious, I hope," Justin replied. There was a strange gleam in his eyes that gave Quinn a funny feeling in the pit of his stomach. It was almost as if Justin was amused by the idea of Quinn getting hurt and needing medical attention.

"Nothing a little rest won't fix," Quinn said. Time to end this conversation. He started to push the door closed. "I hope you enjoyed your visit to the park. Sorry we didn't get a chance to meet up. Have a safe trip home."

Justin smiled—it was a sly, knowing look that made Quinn's stomach turn. He couldn't get rid of this man soon enough. But just before the door closed, Justin thrust the toe of his shoe into the gap between the door and the jamb.

Quinn glanced up, alarm bells ringing in his head. "What the hell?"

Justin cocked his head to the side. "I told you I wanted to come inside. It's time you let me."

Quinn pushed, but Justin thrust his shoulder against the wood of the door. Quinn's injuries had sapped some of his strength; he was no match for Justin's determined assault. Quinn stumbled back, pain lighting up his side and back as he watched Justin stride into his apartment like he owned the place.

Where's the gun? He hadn't had a chance to unpack the bags from the ill-advised camping trip. His pistol should still be stashed in his pack, but where was it?

Quinn glanced around, trying to keep one eye on Justin as he searched for the bags. Rebecca had carried them in, but where had she put them?

"Nice place," Justin commented casually.

"What do you want?" Quinn planted his feet and crossed his arms. Whatever Justin had planned, he knew it wasn't good. Glancing past Justin's shoulder, Quinn spied the blue fabric of his backpack in the corner; now he just had to think of a way to get the bag without raising suspicion.

Justin pushed up the sleeves of his shirt, revealing a few deep red scratches on his forearms. As soon as Quinn saw them, his heart dropped.

"You're the one who attacked me."

Justin nodded but didn't speak.

Quinn connected the rest of the dots. "You're the Yoga Killer." It wasn't a question—Quinn knew it was the truth as soon as he'd said the words.

Justin smiled, clearly pleased. "The one and only," he said. He bowed slightly, as if acknowledging applause.

Shock and revulsion filled Quinn, making his stomach turn. "Why?" He thought back to his interactions with Justin before Ashley and Naomi had died. He'd never been friends with the man, but they'd been on friendly terms. Justin had always seemed a little strange, but Quinn had never imagined he'd turn out to be a serial killer.

Shows how much I know.

He heard Rebecca's voice in his ear, remembered their conversation about the monsters that walked undetected in the crowd. It seemed Quinn had found one, but he hadn't the first idea what to do about it.

Justin cocked his head to the side, studying Quinn. "You really haven't figured that part out?"

Quinn simply shook his head, unsure of what to say.

Justin narrowed his eyes as he took a step closer. "Use your imagination. What could have possibly happened in my life that would make me want to hurt you?"

"Naomi."

"Don't say her name!" Justin's hand disappeared behind his back, returning a second later with a gun.

Quinn held up his hands, palms out. "Okay, okay," he said soothingly. "I won't talk about her." Justin had come here to kill him, that much was clear. But if Quinn could keep him calm, he might stand a chance of defending himself.

"You took her from me." Justin's words were clipped, forced out between his clenched teeth. "You killed her, and you were never punished for it."

Quinn took a half step to the side, inching closer toward the bag. Justin tracked his movement, the gun still down at his side. But Quinn knew that could change in an instant. He had to get his own gun before Justin decided to start shooting…

"You weren't the only one who lost your wife that day," he said. He tried to keep the anger out of his voice, but it was no use. "Ashley died, too."

"And whose fault is that?" Justin snapped. "You were supposed to be hiking with them. You were supposed to keep them safe." He pointed with the gun, his eyes wild with emotion. "For all I know, you set the whole thing up to look like an accident."

"Why would I do that?" Quinn said, risking another half step toward the bag. "I loved Ashley. I never wanted to hurt her."

"Maybe not," Justin said. "But you were always jealous of her relationship with Naomi. I know you hated it when they would spend time together."

Quinn gaped at Justin, at a loss for words. Where was Justin getting this from? He had never begrudged Ashley's friendship with Naomi—on the contrary, he'd been happy the women had been able to spend time together. But he knew any protestations would only further anger Justin and possibly provoke him into shooting.

"I don't think you meant to kill Ashley that day," Justin continued.

"Oh?" Another step. Getting closer…

"I think you meant for them to have an accident, but that you intended to save Ashley before she could be seriously hurt."

Under any other circumstances, the accusation would have made Quinn's blood boil. But he was so intent on getting to the bag that he barely registered the words. Besides, he wasn't going to let himself be provoked by a lunatic.

"You're saying I murdered Naomi."

"I know you did," Justin countered. "You pushed both women off the ledge, trying to make it look like an accident." He took a step forward, lifting the gun. "Don't try to deny it."

Quinn kept his mouth shut, his heart pounding in his chest. A drop of sweat ran down the valley of his spine, and he wiped his palms on his pants. "All right," he said, swallowing hard. "I won't."

Justin stared at him, and for a split second, Quinn thought this was it. He half expected Justin to shoot him between the eyes, but instead he gestured to the recliner. "Have a seat."

Quinn considered arguing, but decided against it. If he sat maybe Justin would, too. If he could get the other man to relax, he might let his guard down enough that Quinn could get to the gun.

It was a chance he would have to take. He sank into the chair, keeping his eyes on Justin. *Sit down,* he silently urged.

"So you killed those women to punish me?" He needed to keep Justin talking, keep his mind off the gun in his hand. Quinn knew he couldn't distract him forever, but every moment counted.

Justin nodded. "My original intention was to frame you for their murders. I knew you'd never do time for killing Naomi, but I hoped I could still put you in prison." He shrugged. "Then I realized you'd fallen in love, so I changed my mind." He reached into his pocket and withdrew a silencer, which he screwed onto the muzzle of the gun.

A cold chill gripped Quinn's heart. "What do you

mean? I'm not in love." But the words sounded false even to his own ears.

Justin smiled maliciously. "Oh? That's not what you said last night."

"Last night?" Quinn asked.

"I was in your hospital room," Justin confirmed. "I'd come there to kill you. Imagine my surprise when I found that woman in your hospital bed."

"She's just a friend," Quinn said, his mouth dry.

"I don't think so." Justin shook his head. "You woke up briefly, and I asked if she was your wife. Do you remember what you told me?"

Quinn shook his head, but Justin didn't wait for his reply. "You said, 'Not yet.'" He laughed softly. "Not yet. That's when I realized you were in love with her. I knew you wanted her when I saw you both at the bar that night, but I figured that was just sexual attraction. I had no idea you'd fall for her so quickly."

Me, neither. But Quinn remained silent. What was there to say? Denying his feelings for Rebecca wasn't going to fool Justin. Her face danced through his mind's eye and he realized with a heavy heart that he was probably going to die before he could confess his love for her.

The thought filled him with anger and his hands curled into fists. Was he really going to sit here passively while this man tried to take away the only happiness he'd known since Ashley's death?

No. He wasn't going to just roll over and die. He wanted to see Rebecca's face again. To smell her hair and feel her cheek as he held her close. He wanted her to hear him say the words *I love you*. He wanted to spend the rest of his life with her.

Hopefully, it would be a long one.

Quinn's muscles tensed in anticipation. He'd have one chance to surprise Justin—he had to make it count.

"Don't even think about it," Justin said. He pointed the gun at Quinn's knee with a knowing smirk. "If you so much as breathe heavy, I'm going to shoot you. Is that what you want?"

"Why don't you just kill me now?" Quinn asked. "Why are you dragging this out?"

"Oh, I'll kill you soon enough," Justin replied. "But only after the whole gang is here."

A sudden, horrible clarity descended over him. "No," Quinn protested. He tried to shout the word, but it came out as a whisper. "Leave her out of this. She's innocent."

"So was Naomi," Justin said. His voice was heavy with pain, and Quinn realized that in spite of all his evil deeds, Justin was still grieving the loss of his wife.

"Justin, why does another woman have to die? This is between you and me—you don't need to include anyone else."

"Nice try." Justin shook his head. "But she's part of this now. Nothing you can do or say will change that." He aimed the gun at Quinn's chest and settled onto the sofa across from him. "Now be quiet. We shouldn't have to wait too long."

Chapter 16

"That's not like you, Rebecca." Frank's tone over the phone was a mixture of surprise and concern, tinged with a hint of disappointment. "Your instincts have never been so wrong before."

Rebecca sighed, knowing her boss was right. "I don't know what's wrong with me," she said. She glanced around, but she needn't have worried. The corridor outside the police chief's office was empty, giving her a modicum of privacy.

Frank made a thoughtful hum, and she pictured him standing in his office, staring out the window. "This case has been different from the start," he said. "Your reports have reflected that."

She nodded, even though he couldn't see her. "I really thought Harry was the guy."

"I know. It was an honest mistake."

His absolution made her feel marginally better, but Rebecca knew it would be a long time before she could close her eyes without being haunted by the memory of the last victim. "I need your advice," she said. "You've seen all the files, read all my reports. What am I missing?"

"I'm not sure," Frank replied. He sounded rueful. "I probably would have come to the same conclusion you did. The fact that there's no other obvious suspect makes me think you haven't encountered him yet."

"That's what I'm afraid of," Rebecca confessed. "If I haven't scooped him up yet, I might not be able to. He's probably long gone by now."

"No," Frank said. "I don't think so. The last murder was a break from his pattern. He's losing control. The smart thing to do would be to leave, but he's not going to be able to see that. He's got a plan, and the encounter with Quinn shook him up. He's going to try to course correct, and that's when he'll make a mistake."

"You sound pretty sure of that," Rebecca said. "I wish I shared your confidence."

Frank chuckled. "I've been doing this for a long time," he said. "You learn a few things."

"So I'm basically stuck in a holding pattern until he makes the next move."

"Not necessarily," Frank replied. "He's already

feeling uncertain and insecure. Capitalize on that. Step up your efforts, really shake the trees. Increase the publicity surrounding the case. He'll know you're coming for him. It might scare him into making a move."

Rebecca considered his suggestion. She remained quiet for so long that Frank spoke up again. "You still there?"

"I don't know if I can handle another death on my conscience," she said softly. "I hate the idea of provoking him into killing another woman."

"You can't control his actions," Frank said. "Whatever he does, it's not your fault."

"Tell that to the family of Olivia Parsons."

"You're taking this one personally. Why?"

It was a question she'd asked herself repeatedly. Even before Olivia's death, Rebecca had felt emotionally invested in this case in a way that she usually didn't. She thought it might have something to do with Quinn. It had been clear from the start that the perpetrator had a vendetta against Quinn, and since Rebecca had fallen in love with him, it was hard not to take the killer's actions personally.

But she couldn't very well explain that to Frank. She'd already given him reason to suspect her professional judgment. The last thing she needed was to confess she'd started a relationship with a man who was part of her investigation.

"It's hard not to take it personally when the last victim was found in my tent," she said tersely.

"Fair enough," Frank replied. "But you've got to get your professional distance back, or you'll burn out fast. I don't need to tell you how dangerous it is to let these guys get under your skin."

"I know." It was one of the biggest risks of her job. If she couldn't maintain a separation between herself and her cases, she'd lose her ability to work. Every time she started an investigation, she put herself in danger of becoming one of the victims—not in the physical sense, but psychologically speaking. She knew a handful of people who hadn't been able to shake off the horrors—they'd retired, but were still haunted by the things they'd seen and heard.

It was a fate she wanted to avoid. She was going to have to ignore her feelings for Quinn and put on her emotional armor once again. It was the only way to protect herself.

"Call me if you need anything," Frank said. "And keep me posted."

"Will do." She ended the call and sat in silence, her mind wandering as she tried to plan her next move. Time to call a press conference, maybe grant a few in-depth interviews to some of the local reporters...

Her phone buzzed in her hand, and she checked the display.

I need to go back to the hospital.

Her heart jumped into her throat as she read the message from Quinn. What had happened to him?

When she'd left, he'd seemed fine. Had he fallen, or done something to open up his wounds? Or maybe he needed more blood… Her imagination kicked into overdrive, conjuring up various scenarios, each more dire than the last.

She grabbed her bag and took off down the hall, not bothering to say goodbye to the police chief. She typed out a message on her way to the car.

On my way.

"Hold on, Quinn," she muttered, climbing behind the wheel. "Just hold on."

Quinn heard Rebecca's footsteps pounding down the hallway and knew she must be running toward the door. A wave of love washed over him as he pictured her—she must have dropped everything when she'd gotten the text Justin had sent.

Justin heard the sound as well and smiled. "Showtime," he said softly.

Quinn took a deep breath as the key scraped in the lock. "Stay back!" he yelled. It was his last chance to warn Rebecca about the danger in his apartment. He didn't expect her to leave, but at least she wouldn't be caught totally unaware.

Justin frowned. "Idiot," he muttered. "You'll pay for that."

There was a pause, then Rebecca pushed the door open and walked inside. She glanced at him, her expression shuttered. Then she looked back at Justin. "So it's you," she said calmly. "I should have known."

Justin pointed the gun at her and gestured for her to take a seat on the couch. When she didn't move, Justin pointed the gun at Quinn. "Do I really have to tell you how this is going to work?"

She shook her head and moved to the sofa. "I've seen enough movies, thank you."

Justin pressed his lips together. "I suppose you think you're clever." Before she could respond, Justin pointed the gun at Quinn and pulled the trigger. Quinn heard a muffled "pop" and his shoulder exploded in a starburst of pain as the breath punched out of his chest.

Rebecca cried out and then he felt her hands on him, pressing hard on his shoulder. Quinn tried to make eye contact with her, but she was focused on his injury and wouldn't look at him. "Go," he choked out in a whisper. "Run now and I'll distract him." He had to make sure she got away from Justin, even if it was the last thing he did.

"Hush," she said. "It's going to be okay."

"You do know I can hear you, right?" Justin asked loudly.

Quinn ignored him, focusing only on Rebecca's face. He wasn't going to waste what might be his last moments on earth with the woman he loved by acknowledging the psycho in the room.

She glanced at him, worry shining in her eyes despite her brave words. Quinn tried to smile. "I love you," he said softly. It was the worst time in the world to confess his feelings for her, but he might not get another chance.

Rebecca blinked, clearly surprised by his unexpected declaration.

"Now we're getting somewhere," Justin said. He leaned forward, putting his face close to Quinn's. "I knew I was right."

Rebecca turned her head and gave Justin a level stare. "You know, I walked in here intending to arrest you. But now I think I'm going to have to kill you."

Her words shocked Quinn. Rebecca was a model professional, the type of agent who always kept her head. Was she bluffing? Or had Justin's actions pushed her over the edge?

Quinn couldn't let her sacrifice her principles like that. He shook his head, trying to communicate with her. But she was so focused on Justin she didn't notice him.

Justin merely smirked and pointed the gun at her. "You sound pretty confident for a woman who's unarmed."

"I like my chances."

Justin opened his mouth to respond, but was interrupted by a pounding on the door. "Quinn? Are you okay? I heard a loud bang from your apartment."

Quinn's heart sank as he registered the voice. It was Mrs. Shepherd, the widow who lived two doors down. She was a retired elementary school teacher, and she had made it her mission in life to look after him. She routinely brought him casseroles and freshly baked bread, and in return he carried her groceries and helped her with any minor maintenance issues that cropped up. He considered her a friend; the last thing he wanted was for her to be on Justin's radar.

Justin glanced at him, one eyebrow raised. Quinn cleared his throat and raised his voice. "I'm fine," he said, trying to sound normal. "It must have come from outside."

The older woman was quiet, making Quinn think she'd gone back to her apartment. "What's wrong with you? Are you hurt?"

"No," Quinn yelled. *Just go home*, he pleaded silently. This was rapidly spiraling out of control…

"I'm calling the police," the woman said firmly.

Justin grabbed Rebecca roughly by the arm, hauling her to her feet. They started for the door, his gun pressed to her jaw as they walked.

"No, Mrs. Shepherd." Ignoring the pain in his shoulder, Quinn struggled to his feet. He couldn't save himself, and he might not be able to save Rebecca, but he could hopefully save Mrs. Shepherd from an untimely death.

"Open up and let me see you," the older woman insisted. "If I can see you're all right, I won't call the police."

Justin paused at the door. He glanced back, noticed Quinn had moved. He dug the muzzle of the gun into Rebecca's neck, his meaning clear. Quinn stopped, his hand on the wall for support.

Justin reached for the door handle and Quinn looked down, unable to watch him shoot an innocent woman. Shame and self-loathing filled him as he realized he wasn't a hero after all. He hadn't been able to save Ashley, and now he couldn't save Rebecca.

Or could he?

His breath snagged as he realized where he was, and what he was looking at.

The backpack sat at his feet. The unobtrusive bag represented his last hope of protecting Rebecca and putting an end to Justin's madness. But would the gun even work?

There was only one way to find out.

Quinn sank to his knees.

"Let me talk to her," Rebecca said in a low voice. "I can get her to leave."

"Oh?" Justin's grip on her arm tightened. "Why should I let you?"

"If you shoot her, that will alert everyone in the building. Someone will call the police, and you'll have to run before they arrive. I know you want to spend time torturing me and Quinn before killing us, but you won't be able to do that if you don't exercise a little patience now."

She held her breath as Justin considered her words. She knew he had the self-control to resist killing Quinn's neighbor. But his thirst for blood was high, and shooting Quinn had only served to whet his appetite for violence. Would he be able to resist the temptation of another helpless victim?

Finally, he nodded. "Don't try anything," he warned, his breath hot in her ear. "Or I will make sure her death is painful."

He shoved her in front of the door and reached for the handle. The muzzle of the gun was nestled between her ribs, lest she forget what was at stake.

Rebecca took a breath and mussed her hair. She untucked and partially unbuttoned her shirt, then opened the door a crack, positioning herself in the gap to keep the woman from seeing inside the apartment. "Hi," she said, injecting false cheer into her voice. "Quinn is a bit, um, indisposed at the moment, so he asked me to assure you everything is fine."

A petite woman stared up at her, her blue eyes bright behind round glasses. "Is that so?"

Rebecca smiled. "Yes, ma'am." She leaned forward, dropping her voice to a conspiratorial whisper. "I'm taking good care of him." She winked, and the older woman blushed.

"I see." The neighbor adjusted her glasses, rocking back on her heels a bit. "Well. Well, I suppose that's none of my business." She took a step back, clearly uncomfortable. "I'm sorry for bothering you."

"No worries," Rebecca said. "I'll tell Quinn to stop by later."

"That won't be necessary," the woman said, halfway to her door at this point. She practically dove into her apartment, the door slamming shut behind her.

Rebecca closed Quinn's door with a sigh of relief. One hurdle down. Now she just needed to figure out a way to distract Justin long enough to reach the gun in her ankle holster…

Justin grabbed her arm again, his fingers digging into her bicep. He forced her to turn around and they both froze at the sight that greeted them.

Quinn stood in the doorway to the living room, a gun in his hand.

What the hell? Rebecca's first, absurd thought was to wonder where he had gotten a gun. Her second thought was to wonder if he would be able to use it.

Quinn's left hand shook a bit as he aimed the gun at Justin. His right arm hung useless at his side, blood dripping from his fingers as he took a step forward. She knew Quinn was right-handed, but did Justin realize that?

Justin jerked Rebecca hard to the side, pulling her in front of him to use her body as a shield. He pressed the muzzle of his gun to the corner of her jaw. "Drop it," he said. "Or I'll shoot her."

Quinn met her eyes, as if seeking guidance. *I'm okay*, she mouthed. Justin might eventually make good on his threat to shoot her, but she didn't think he'd do it right away. At least, she hoped not…

"Let her go," Quinn countered. "This is between you and me. Why don't you act like a man and stop hiding behind an innocent woman?"

Good one, she silently cheered. Unless she missed her guess, a big part of Justin's pathology centered around the impotence he'd felt regarding his wife's death. Quinn was tapping into that feeling, which would only serve to distract Justin from her plan.

Moving carefully, Rebecca lifted her right leg and ran her hand down the side of her calf. Justin was so focused on Quinn he didn't notice her actions, but she could tell by the subtle widening of Quinn's eyes that he realized what she was doing.

"Why don't you point that gun at me?" Quinn suggested. "I'm your true target."

"Scared I'll hurt her?" Justin said. "You should be."

Rebecca tugged her pant leg up and began to fumble blindly at the holster strapped to her ankle. In a matter of seconds, she had the gun in her hand. The feel of the cold metal against her skin was comforting, and a wave of confidence washed over her. She no longer felt powerless and scared—now she had the upper hand.

But Justin didn't know it yet.

She thumbed off the safety and reached around her torso, tucking the barrel of the gun against her side so that it pointed at Justin. She didn't know where exactly he'd be hit, but at this range, she couldn't miss.

"Drop your weapon," she said, giving him one last chance to comply. *Please, don't let there be anyone standing in the hallway...* The last thing she wanted was for the bullet to pass through Justin and hit an innocent bystander.

Justin responded by moving his gun from her jaw

to her temple. "I'm in charge here," he said angrily. "Don't forget that."

"Not anymore," she muttered. Rebecca closed her eyes and pulled the trigger.

The gunshot sounded like a cannon in the confines of the hallway. Justin jerked against her, his grip on her arm loosening. She took the opportunity to dive to the floor, away from his gun.

She glanced up to see Justin leaning against the door, a look of blank shock on his face. His shirt sported a rapidly growing bloodstain—it looked like she'd hit him in the abdomen.

Rebecca scooted back a few feet, keeping her gun trained on him. Using the wall for support, she got to her feet. "Drop it," she commanded.

Justin stared at her, then looked at his hand as if surprised to find he was still holding a gun. A gleam of malice entered his eyes, and he aimed at Quinn.

Rebecca fired just as he pulled the trigger. She shot him three times in rapid succession, not stopping until she saw Justin fall back against the door. His limp body slid to the ground with a thud, the light fading from his eyes.

She approached carefully, even though he appeared to be dead. His gun had landed next to his body, so she kicked it away, out of his reach in case he was playing possum. She nudged him with the toe of her boot, but he didn't move. Satisfied he was no longer a threat, Rebecca turned to look at Quinn and her heart stopped.

He was on the floor, his face twisted in pain. She ran to him, skidding to a stop before she crashed into him. "Are you okay? Did he hit you again?" She ran her hands along his body, searching for any new injuries. But his shirt was already bloody from his shoulder, and the wound on his side appeared to have opened up again, making it hard to tell if Justin's final volley had found its mark.

Quinn shook his head. "I don't think so. I dropped to the ground when he fired, and I think he missed me."

Relief washed over her as she verified the truth of his words for herself. "He did," she said, feeling out of breath. "You're okay." She glanced past him to see a bullet hole in the wall next to the window. The brick of the building had likely stopped the bullet, but even if it had made it through, it was unlikely to have hit anyone outside.

"Quinn?" Mrs. Shepherd's voice came through the door again, her tone determined. "I'm calling the police this time. I know those were gunshots."

Rebecca and Quinn looked at each other. Despite the circumstances, a laugh bubbled up in her throat. She tried to hold it back, but it was no use. A giggle escaped, and she clapped her hand over her mouth. Quinn cracked a smile at her reaction. "Okay, Mrs. Shepherd," he said loudly, as Rebecca grabbed her own phone and began dialing the police. "Thanks for looking out for me."

Chapter 17

"I didn't expect to see you here again," Dr. Allen said as she walked into the emergency bay. "Are you trying to turn into one of my frequent fliers?"

Quinn didn't bother to smile at the lame joke. After the events of the afternoon he wanted nothing more than to take Rebecca into his arms and retreat into his bedroom, where they could lock the door and pretend the rest of the world didn't exist.

Unfortunately, that wasn't an option.

It hadn't taken long for the police to arrive, followed by an ambulance. Rebecca had stayed in his apartment to talk to the police, while he'd been loaded onto a gurney and whisked away to the hospital. She'd looked shaken but determined, and he wondered how she was holding up. He knew shooting Justin had been the only way to stop him, but Rebecca had never killed a man before. Was she okay? He hated being separated from her again, but she'd promised to visit as soon as she was able to get away.

But who knew when that would be?

His apartment had been a study in chaos when he'd left—it seemed like there was blood everywhere, and the place had been packed with officers combing through the hallway and living room. He figured it was only a matter of time before the police arrived to interview him as well. He closed his eyes, exhausted by just the thought of reliving the afternoon's events.

"You got lucky," Dr. Allen said. "Looks like the bullet went through your shoulder without hitting anything important. You reopened the wound on your side, though, so that's going to need to be repaired as well. We'll get you patched up and on your way as soon as possible."

"Thanks, doc," he said.

"No problem." She gave his uninjured shoulder a friendly pat. "But this time, I'm serious about you taking it easy. I don't want to see you back here again."

"Nothing personal, but I don't want to see you again, either."

She chuckled. "I'll go grab my supplies. Be back in a minute."

It didn't take long for the doctor to stitch him up, and soon Quinn was alone in a room, hooked to an

IV of fluids and antibiotics Dr. Allen wanted him to have "just in case."

He closed his eyes and sighed, missing Rebecca more than he could say. The worst part of the day hadn't been finding out Justin was the killer, or even getting shot. No, the worst part had been thinking Rebecca was going to die and feeling helpless to stop it.

He needed to see her, to hear her voice and hold her so he could know for certain she was all right. Even though she hadn't been injured in the skirmish, the image of Justin pressing a gun to her temple would haunt him for the rest of his life. Just thinking about it made his palms sweat and his muscles tremble.

"She's fine," he told himself, taking a deep breath. "It's over."

He still couldn't wrap his head around Justin's behavior. What had made the other man think Quinn had deliberately killed Ashley and Naomi? Had he simply needed someone to blame for the loss of his wife? It was an impulse Quinn could understand, but he'd never be able to figure out why Justin had turned that pain outward, targeting innocent women in his elaborate revenge scheme. Quinn knew he wasn't responsible for Justin's actions, but he was a bit unsettled to know those women were dead because Justin had wanted to punish him. It was a thought that was going to haunt him for a long time...

But what would happen now? What did the future have in store for him, and for his relationship with Rebecca? Could he really return to his work as a park ranger without being plagued by visions of the women Justin had killed?

But what other choice did he have? He loved being a park ranger. If he quit to find another job, it would be one more thing Justin had wrecked. Even though it would be difficult, Quinn refused to be his victim a third time.

But what did that mean for him and Rebecca? Could they find a way to make a long-distance relationship work? Or were they destined to burn hot and bright, fizzling out in a matter of weeks?

His musings were interrupted by a rap on the door. Rebecca?

"Come in," he called out, his heart in his throat.

The door opened, but it wasn't Rebecca. Two officers entered the room and introduced themselves.

"We'd like to get your statement regarding the events in your apartment this afternoon."

"No problem," Quinn said, trying to mask his disappointment. He'd known this was coming, and talking to the police would help pass the time until Rebecca arrived.

He talked to them for a couple of hours, going over all the details and answering their questions as best he could. The detectives listened intently, interrupting only to ask for clarification of some points.

As Quinn spoke, the residual tension from the final standoff with Justin gradually left his body. The knowledge that Justin was dead and this nightmare was well and truly over settled into his bones.

For the first time in what felt like months, Quinn re-laxed, body and soul.

The detectives had just asked another question when there was a knock on the door. "Yes?" Quinn called out. He tried not to get his hopes up, as it was probably a doctor or one of the nurses coming to check on him.

The door opened and Rebecca poked her head inside. "Feel up for a visitor?"

His heart soared at the sight of her, and he couldn't stop a grin from spreading across his face. "If it's you? Anytime."

She smiled back, and for a second they were the only two people in the world.

One of the officers cleared his throat, ending the moment. "Oh!" Twin pink spots appeared on Rebecca's cheeks. "I'm sorry. I didn't mean to interrupt."

"We're finishing up," said one of the officers.

It took longer than he liked, but soon enough the two detectives said their goodbyes and Quinn and Rebecca were alone together.

She walked to the edge of the bed, staring down at him with emotions swirling in her blue eyes. "Are you really okay?" she asked. "I didn't get to talk to your doctor this time."

"I'm fine," he assured her.

"Can I touch you?" She sounded a little shy, which made him laugh.

"I know it sounds funny, but I need to touch you to convince myself you're fine."

"I understand," he said. "Of course you can touch me. You don't have to ask for permission first."

She made a face. "Well, I don't want to hurt you. Where's a safe spot?"

He gave her a suggestive smile and she laughed. "Okay, I set myself up there." Leaning forward, she cupped his face with her hands. "I don't want to insult your masculine pride, but I hardly think now's the time for such activities."

She kissed him then, softly and sweetly. Her mouth was warm, her lips welcoming. He reached for her, only to draw back with a yelp as the movement pulled on his IV.

"Damn," he muttered.

Rebecca gave him a sympathetic smile. "You're not the only one who's disappointed."

He scooted over in the bed. "Have a seat," he said, patting the mattress. If he couldn't kiss her, he could at least be close to her.

She sat facing him, her leg pressed against his outer thigh. "I feel like we've done this before," she joked.

"It does seem familiar," he said.

She was quiet a moment. Based on her expression he could tell she was thinking, and he didn't want to interrupt. He was content to look at her, drinking in the sight of her the way a starving man might gaze at a plate of food.

"Did you mean it?" Her question caught him off guard and he shook his head.

"Did I mean what?" Quinn wasn't sure what she was talking about, but he knew from her tone it was serious.

"In your apartment," she clarified. "After Justin shot you. I was applying pressure to your shoulder and you told me you loved me. Did you mean it?"

"Oh," he said dumbly. He felt his cheeks burn and knew he must be blushing.

"Yes, I meant it," he said, meeting her gaze. His heart was beating in his chest like a kettle drum as his nerves took hold. "It wasn't a lie, or a ploy to manipulate Justin. I do love you. I had hoped to tell you under different circumstances, but…" He trailed off, shrugging his good shoulder.

Rebecca's eyes were bright. "I hoped you were telling the truth." She grabbed his hand, squeezing tightly.

"That's encouraging," he said teasingly.

She smiled. "I love you, too. I don't know how it happened, but somewhere along the way I realized I need you in my life."

A large lump formed in Quinn's throat, threatening to choke him. He swallowed hard. "I feel the same way about you." It wasn't the most eloquent response, but it was the best he could do at the moment.

He opened his arms and she leaned forward, snuggling against his chest with her cheek pressed to his heart. They fit together perfectly, like two puzzle pieces custom-made for each other. Quinn stroked Rebecca's hair, a sense of peace stealing over him as he held the woman he loved.

He wasn't sure how much time passed. He could have stayed that way forever, but Rebecca eventually sat up. "So what happens now? Where do we go from here?"

Quinn shook his head. "I'm not sure. But I do know that I want us to be together."

"So do I," Rebecca said. "But how can we make that work? Your job is here. Mine is across the country. That seems like a pretty big obstacle."

"It's a problem," Quinn conceded. "But we don't have to have all the answers figured out now, do we? Can't we work on things as we go?"

"I suppose we'll have to," Rebecca said. There was a strange note in her voice—a hint of defeat, or perhaps fatalism.

A spike of fear pierced his heart. Was she already having second thoughts?

"Hey." Quinn waited until she met his gaze again. "What's wrong?"

She smiled ruefully. "Am I that obvious?"

"Only to me."

Rebecca nodded. "I'm just worried," she said with a sigh. "You're the first man I've loved since Brandon's death. I don't want to lose you. But I don't know how this is going to work in the long run."

It was the same issue that had troubled him since he'd recognized his feelings for Rebecca. But despite all his thinking on the subject, he still didn't have a satisfactory solution.

"I can't answer that." He shook his head, hating

to think they might be over even before they really gave things a chance. "I'm not going to try to convince you to give us a go. You need to want this as much as I do. I'll understand if you don't." It was a lie—he'd be broken-hearted if she ended things here, but he wasn't going to play on her emotions. If they were going to try a long-distance relationship, they both had to be all in.

Rebecca shook her head. "You're not getting rid of me that easily," she said. "I told you before—I love you. I want to see where this goes."

Quinn nearly laughed in relief. "Okay," he said. "Then we will. But promise me this—we take things one day at a time. Don't go worrying about the unknown future. Just focus on the here and now. Can you do that for me?"

Rebecca smiled. "I think I can handle that. But I might need you to help distract me." She lifted her eyebrows suggestively and Quinn laughed.

"I know a few things we can do to keep your mind sufficiently occupied," he said.

She winked and leaned forward, planting a hot kiss on his lips that left him breathless and yearning for more. "I'm counting on it."

Six weeks later

"Are you sure you want to do this?"

Rebecca smiled at her boss. "I'm only taking a couple of weeks off. I'll be back."

The older man frowned, not trying to hide his re-action. "Are you sure? Because it kind of feels like you're gearing up to leave. I'd hate to lose you. You're one of my best."

Rebecca tucked another book into her bag. "I haven't decided that yet. And besides, even if I did move on, you'll find others. You know there's always a group of young kids waiting in the wings to replace us older veterans."

Frank snorted. "You're not old. Not by a long shot."

"Maybe not. But I *feel* old. And that's reason enough for me to take a vacation."

Her boss sighed. "If you're sure that's all it is?"

Rebecca nodded. In truth, Frank wasn't too far off the mark. She was considering a change in course. It would be nice to take a step back from profiling work, go in a different direction. One that would allow her to be closer to Quinn…

"All right. Just promise me you'll give me a heads-up before you make any rash decisions?"

She nodded, feeling a little lump in her throat. She knew Frank cared for her, and she considered him a friend. If she did decide to transfer, she would miss him terribly.

Frank cleared his throat and nodded. "Enjoy your time off then. I hope you find the answers you're searching for." He hesitated, then gave her shoulder a pat as he walked out of her office.

Rebecca smiled. Had it been up to her, she would

have hugged him. But she knew Frank wouldn't appreciate such an overt physical display.

She packed up a few more files and carried her bag down to her car. Technically, her vacation didn't start until Friday, but she had to admit that mentally, she was already out the door.

Her thoughts wandered as she drove home, landing as they so often did on Quinn. *I wonder what he's doing right now?* She thought about calling him, but decided to wait. It was the middle of the afternoon, and he'd still be at work. She'd talk to him tonight, when they'd have more time to chat.

The past six weeks had been better than she'd expected. The distance had been challenging, but every other weekend they had made time to see each other. Quinn had come to Virginia first, then she had gone back to Alpine. Their visits were never long enough, but it was better than nothing.

Quinn had enjoyed his first trip to Virginia. Rebecca had worried that the time apart would make things a little awkward, but as soon as they saw each other it was like they'd never been separated. They'd spent all of Saturday in bed, talking and laughing and making love, only coming up for air to eat. She'd taken him out on Sunday, showing him a bit of the area before putting him back on a plane to Texas. Saying goodbye had broken her heart a little, but the knowledge that she was going to Alpine in a couple of weeks had softened the blow.

Her trip to see Quinn had been a little tougher

than she'd anticipated. Seeing him had been wonderful, but she'd had a hard time going to his apartment. Being back in that space reminded her of Justin and that horrible afternoon, when she'd almost lost Quinn.

He'd noticed her reaction. "I'm moving soon," he'd told her. "I hate living here now."

They hadn't talked about that day, choosing instead to focus on each other and the time they had together. But Rebecca hadn't stopped thinking about the case, and she began to wonder if perhaps she might be happier doing something else.

Truth be told, she'd been wondering if profiling work was really the right fit for her. She was good at her job—or at least, she'd felt that way until she'd mistakenly identified Harry as the killer. But it wasn't just a crisis of confidence that had her rethinking everything. Losing Brandon and finding love again with Quinn had triggered a tectonic shift in her life, causing her to reevaluate her priorities. Spending more time with Quinn had convinced her that he was the man for her. But she couldn't make him and their relationship a priority if she remained committed to a job she no longer enjoyed.

So she was seriously thinking about putting in her notice at work and applying for a teaching position in Texas. The university in El Paso was looking for someone to spearhead the development of a forensic psychology program, which sounded right up her alley. And while El Paso was several hours away from Alpine and Big Bend, she figured she and Quinn could make it work. She wouldn't mind the commute, if it meant coming home to him at the end of every day.

She pulled in to her driveway, frowning as she noticed a man sitting on her front porch. That was odd. Then he stood, and she realized with a shock it was Quinn.

Joy filled her at the unexpected sight of him. She parked and got out of the car as fast as she could. He met her in the driveway, drawing her close for a hug. He bent his head and kissed her, making her toes curl in anticipation.

"What are you doing here?" She reached up to touch the side of his face, rubbing her fingertip over the stubble on his cheek. "Not that I'm complaining. But I didn't expect you until Friday."

He grinned. "I've been doing some thinking, and I couldn't wait to talk to you."

"I could say the same thing to you." She hadn't told him about her idea to move yet. She'd wanted it to be a surprise. But now that he was here, she had to share.

She led him inside the house and they sat on the sofa together. "You go first," he said. Excitement danced in his brown eyes and she couldn't help but smile. It was so good to see him happy again—over the past few weeks, he'd lost the haunted look that had seemed to be lurking just under the surface after Justin's attack on them both. Rebecca was glad to see the changes in him; Justin's ghost had no place in their lives.

She took a deep breath. "Well," she began, feeling suddenly self-conscious, "I'm thinking about quitting my job. There's an open position at the university in El Paso, and I'm willing to pack up and move to Texas so we can be together."

Quinn's expression was a mixture of shock and disbelief. "Are you serious?"

Rebecca nodded, feeling a prickle of unease at his reaction. "I am." When he didn't say anything, she prodded. "I can't tell if you think that's a good thing or not."

Quinn shook his head and laughed. "Oh, I think it's a great thing, if you're sure that's what you really want. But why do you want to quit? I thought you loved working as a profiler."

She shrugged. "Not so much anymore. I'm glad I did it for so long, but I'm starting to think the job no longer fits me, if that makes any sense."

"It does." Quinn squeezed her hand. "I'm proud of you for being willing to make a change. I know how hard that is."

"Tell me about your news," she said. "We can talk more about my changes later. I want to know what's going on with you."

A strange expression crossed his face. "Oh. Uh, I think my revelation is going to be a bit anticlimactic after that, but okay." He reached out to brush a loose strand of hair behind her ear. "I'm ready to apply for a transfer."

Rebecca felt a smile tug at the corners of her mouth. "A transfer? Where to?"

"Virginia," Quinn replied. "You guys have a lot of parks and monuments up here. I figured there are plenty of options for a park ranger like myself."

"Are you wanting to do that just for me? Or do you truly want to move?" It seemed they were both looking for a change, but she wanted to make sure Quinn wasn't uprooting his life because he thought she needed him to.

"It's time," he said. His words eased the knot of tension in her stomach. "I enjoyed working in Big Bend, and I'll always have a soft spot for the park. But it holds too many tough memories for me now. I want to move on, to find a place that isn't so…emotionally complicated."

"I totally get that." It was amazing how closely their motivations mirrored each other's. *More proof we're meant to be together*, she thought.

"But I don't have to move here," he said. "If you get the job in El Paso, I can apply to work at a park closer to the city."

"And I don't have to move to El Paso," she said. "If you want to stay in Virginia, there are things I can do here. I could get a teaching position at the FBI academy in Quantico."

"So we both have a lot of options," he said.

They stared at each other for a moment, then Rebecca burst out laughing. "Why do I get the feeling I'm in an O. Henry story?"

Quinn frowned, but his expression cleared quickly. "'The Gift of the Magi'?" he asked.

She nodded. "That's the one."

"If I remember correctly, the story has a happy ending," he said.

"It does," she agreed. "Which is the best kind."

They smiled at each other, and Rebecca's heart felt so full she thought it might burst.

"Well," she said, "it seems as if we're getting a fresh start. What should we do with it?"

"I'm not sure," Quinn said. He pulled her into his arms, and she snuggled against his chest. "But I know one thing—I'll be happy as long as I'm with you."

Rebecca smiled up at him, feeling full of hope for their future together. "I couldn't have said it better myself."

* * * * *

*Look out for future installments in
the Rangers of Big Bend series,
coming soon from
Harlequin Romantic Suspense!*

*And don't miss
Colton K-9 Bodyguard
by Lara Lacombe,
available now from
Harlequin Romantic Suspense!*

"I just wish I had some idea who it is, and why."

"Yeah, me, too." Doug had a sudden urge to take Elissa into his arms, hold her tightly against him, maybe attempt to cheer her a little by kissing that alluring yet sad mouth of hers…

But of course he wouldn't do that. Never mind that he felt attracted to her, or that he wanted to fix things for her. He had plenty of reasons not to get involved with her other than as a civilian who needed help. But she did happen to be a civilian who needed help.

A vision of his uncle Cy's face flashed in his mind, encouraging him and Maisie to become cops like him—and to act like professionals at all times.

"Anyway," she said, "I'll be working at my local hospital tomorrow and Sunday, both as a nurse and doing therapy dog work, so I won't be home much this weekend. Then I'll head back up to Chance on Monday to give my first therapy dog training class. I'll call you then and maybe we can catch up on what's going on here and there."

"All right," Doug conceded. What else could he do? He might be concerned about this attractive, dog-loving civilian, but he wasn't even a cop in the jurisdiction where she lived who could theoretically give her orders—or at least conduct some of those patrols and drop in on her sometimes.

And he clearly wasn't convincing her to do something else—except to walk her dog along with a neighbor. Some of the time. Without additional protection at night.

"Well, be sure to keep in touch." He recognized that his words had come out in a tone of command, which appeared somehow to amuse her.

He wanted to kiss that smile right off her lovely face... but didn't.

He motioned for Hooper to join him at the door, where he removed his dog's leash from his pocket and snapped it on his collar. "Let's go," he told his well-trained partner.

Peace also came to the door to see them off. While they stood there, Elissa petted both dogs. Then, to his surprise, she leaned toward him. "Drive carefully," she said, and planted a soft and swift kiss on his lips before backing away. "And I can't thank you enough for all your help."

You just did, he thought, but all he said was, "You're welcome. Be careful, keep in touch, and we'll see you next week."

Don't miss
Trained to Protect *by Linda O. Johnston,*
available October 2018 wherever
Harlequin® Romantic Suspense books
and ebooks are sold.

www.Harlequin.com

Need an adrenaline rush from nail-biting tales
(and irresistible males)?

Check out **Harlequin Intrigue®**
and **Harlequin® Romantic Suspense** books!

New books available every month!

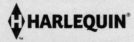

Chapter 10

The next day...

"Why am I here?"

Rebecca closed the door behind her and rounded the table in the small interrogation room. It was the same place she'd first met Quinn, but while he'd been polite and forthcoming, this man was bristling with agitation.

"I have a few questions to ask," she said, taking a seat across from him.

The young man eyed her suspiciously. He was a big guy, built like a linebacker. But his partying life-style was already starting to take a toll; a soft layer of fat covered his muscles, and his eyes were bloodshot. The skin of his cheeks was pink, a fine web of broken capillaries giving him a look of constant embarrassment. She imagined his liver was already in trouble, if it wasn't fully pickled yet.

Peaked in high school, she thought to herself. Football star, maybe even homecoming king. Figured out after graduation that life wasn't always going to be accolades and roses, and the realization made him angry and frustrated. But instead of channeling those emotions into improving himself and his life, he'd chosen to embrace the victim mentality— his lack of success was someone else's fault, and always would be.

His friends had been similar. She'd already spoken to the other two guys, who hadn't given her much. But it was clear this one was the ringleader—whatever he said, they'd probably do.

The question was, had their dissatisfaction turned to murder?

It was possible. Quinn said he'd had several run-ins with this gang, none of them pleasant. If Quinn had tried to enforce park rules, they'd likely taken his words and actions as an insult. Had they built Quinn up in their minds as an enemy to be punished for daring to challenge them? It sounded silly, but people had murdered for less. Emotionally volatile young men like the one before her weren't exactly known for their self-control.

"This is harassment," he said, puffing out his chest. Rebecca smiled pleasantly. "Not quite."